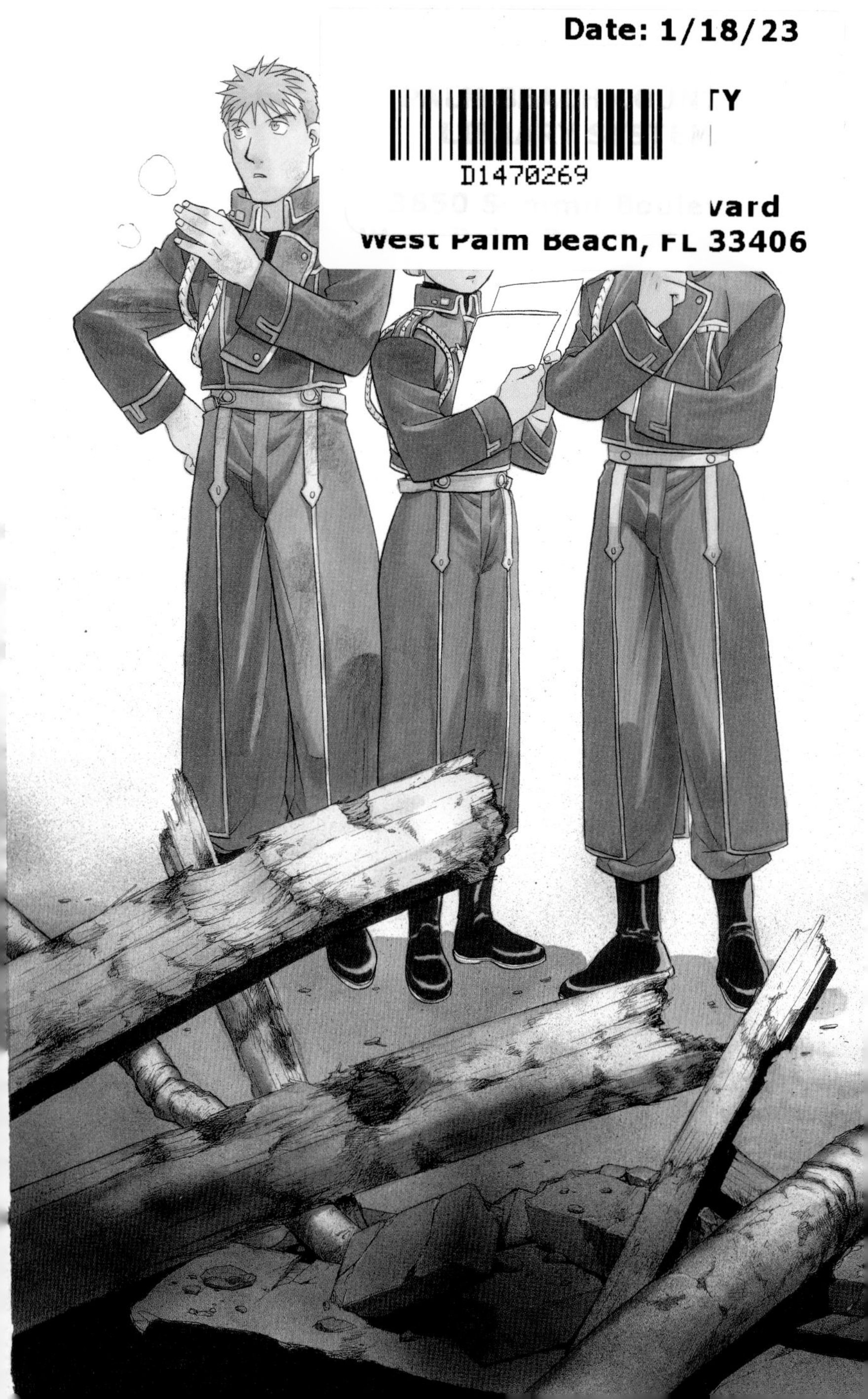

FULLMETAL ALCHEMIST

THE TIES THAT BIND

FULLMETAL ALCHEMIST

THE TIES THAT BIND

Novel by
MAKOTO INOUE

Original concept by
HIROMU ARAKAWA

Translated by
ALEXANDER O. SMITH
with **RICH AMTOWER**

SAN FRANCISCO

FULLMETAL ALCHEMIST
THE TIES THAT BIND

NOVEL FULLMETAL ALCHEMIST VOL. 5 SOREZORE NO KIZUNA
© 2005 Hiromu Arakawa, Makoto Inoue/SQUARE ENIX CO., LTD.
First published in Japan in 2005 by SQUARE ENIX CO., LTD. English translation rights arranged with SQUARE ENIX CO., LTD. and VIZ Media, LLC. English translation © 2022 SQUARE ENIX CO., LTD.

Illustrations: HIROMU ARAKAWA
Cover and interior design: ADAM GRANO
Translation: ALEXANDER O. SMITH with RICH AMTOWER

Published by VIZ Media, LLC
P.O. Box 77010
San Francisco, CA 94107

Library of Congress Cataloging-in-Publication data available.

Printed in Canada
First printing, September 2022

viz.com

CONTENTS
THE TIES THAT BIND

PROLOGUE

DEEP IN THE MOUNTAINS, where roads were few and visitors fewer, stood a lonely mansion.

Vines wound up its walls, and part of the roof had crumbled in. It seemed a building forgotten by time.

A man's voice sounded from within.

"Not yet. Not enough. We still lack materials!"

It was a low, gravelly voice, speaking each word as though incanting a solemn spell.

"My research is nearly complete! Fresh materials . . . We need fresh materials!"

There was a pause, and another voice, far younger, answered with a question.

" . . . You really intend to keep trying?"

"Of course! Now, go. You have the perfect creatures for obtaining the fresh, valuable resources we need, have you not?"

There was no response. The gravelly voice spoke again, this time with a tone of threat lurking just below the surface.

"It is for the good of my research . . . and for your own good as well."

A short while later, the mansion door opened with a shrill screech of rusted metal on metal.

Appearing from within came a man and three chimeras. Behind them, an old man in a white lab coat stood with the help of a staff held in a skinny, wizened hand. His eyes shone with a brilliant light. "Now, go quickly."

The old scientist let the man and the chimeras out, closing the door behind them. He turned back into the room, cackling to himself. "Success, this time, yes! I can smell it!"

Outside, the man stood for a brief moment, listening as the old scientist's unwholesome laughter receded into the distance on the other side of the door. After a short while, he looked up.

". . . Let's go."

With the three chimeras following behind him, the man walked off, disappearing into the woods. ◉

CHAPTER 1

THE BANNED BOOK

A WARM, BRIGHT SUN shone on this town so far from Central City.

People chatted as they walked down streets that stretched beneath a sky tinged brown with dust. Merchants talked to their customers beside busy storefronts. In an empty plot of land, children played tag, their peals of laughter echoing through the buildings.

It was a large town, but unlike in the city, here there were no tense looks or hurried feet. The sound of the conductor's voice calling out the station mingled with the blowing of the whistle.

"Dublith, Dublith . . ."

It was a calm, peaceful moment.

" . . . Yeeeeeeeeaaaaargh!"

An unearthly scream tore through the silence of one peaceful corner of Dublith. Nearby pedestrians stopped in their tracks, looking to see where it had come from. Shortly after followed the sound of something large and metallic clanging to the ground.

In the direction of the sound stood a small shop with a sign that read "MEAT."

"That's enough yowling out of you! On your feet!" A woman stood behind the butcher's shop, chewing out two boys lying on the ground before her.

"Ouch . . . !"

Edward Elric groaned, cradling his head in his hands where he lay in the tall grass.

Edward was a striking boy of fifteen, with long blond hair tied in a braid and eyes the color of gold. His short and wiry frame belied an agile, muscular body, and his fearless gaze somehow managed to be both strong and childlike at once. Yet the dully gleaming automail of his left leg and right arm suggested a surprisingly hard past for one so young.

Next to him, his brother, Alphonse Elric, lay on his back looking up at the sky.

Alphonse, a year younger than Edward, was a kind boy with a gentle manner. Though he appeared at first glance to be wearing a large suit of armor, there was, in fact, nobody inside that suit—only air and a glyph drawn in blood that bound his soul to the metal armor.

The Elric brothers had performed forbidden human transmutation alchemy and earned Edward automail limbs and Alphonse an armored body for their trouble. That was four years ago. Since then, Edward had become a state alchemist. Now he traveled with Alphonse, searching for a way to restore their former bodies.

Though their journey in search of clues into the mysteries of alchemical human transmutation had not been easy, they had seen more and done more than any other children their age, and it had strengthened them in spirit and body. They carried the burden of a hard past on their backs and walked a difficult road—yet most times, they refused to cry or to yield to the challenges they faced.

This, however, was not one of those times.

"Can I just lie here for a while? Maybe, like the whole night?"

"Somehow, I know exactly how you feel, Ed . . ."

The two boys looked up from where they lay on the ground at the woman who, moments before, had casually tossed them through the air.

It was Izumi Curtis, their mentor, the one who had taught both of them alchemy from a young age.

With a simple white dress worn over black trousers and hair bound in braids at the top of her head, Izumi looked like an extremely average housewife. Her bare shoulders were pale, and the ankles that peeked out above her sandals were thin, making the casual observer wonder just where the strength to take down two boys in their prime had come from. She was ill, too—so ill that she regularly coughed up blood and never went far without her medicine.

Though Izumi and "frailty" might rhyme, the two words couldn't be further apart. She had endured severe training in mountains so high they never shed their caps of snow, she had once killed a bear with nothing but a hunting knife, and her skill in martial arts proved more than enough to throw Edward and Alphonse without so much as breaking a sweat.

Few people in the world could make these two boys plead for mercy, but Izumi was one of them.

"Is it just me, or does it seem like she's gotten stronger since we've been gone?"

"I was thinking the same thing! Man, there's tough, and then there's her."

"Stop grousing, and get on your feet!" Izumi barked. "We'll spar once more, and then I want a hundred push-ups, and fifteen miles. Do it, or you'll get no dinner."

"Fifteen miles? You can't be serious . . ." Edward put his hands on the ground, lifting himself to look up. Next to him, Alphonse was sitting half up on the grass, looking dazed.

"It's her. She's always serious."

Back when they had first come to her, asking to become her students, she had tested their abilities by abandoning them on a deserted island for an entire month. Izumi always said "in order to train the mind, you must first train the body," and she stuck to it, making them perform one grueling task after the other.

Edward got to his feet, ready to face her again, when his knees buckled beneath him. "Ahh . . . !" It wasn't hard to understand why. He had been thrown or punched through the air at least thirty-five times already that day.

"C'mon, let's see some hustle! Don't tell me you can't even get up?!"

Izumi stretched out her hand, palm upward, waving her fingers as if to say *come on!*

Edward stood on shaky feet. No matter what troubles faced him, he never gave up. He never backed down, and he wasn't about to start now.

"That all you got?" Edward thrust one foot down and lunged forward, fists raised.

Izumi shook her head. "I don't like your attitude!"

"Yeeaaargh!"

The counterpunch caught Edward in his stomach, and once again he flew up, up into the air, then down, landing with a thud on his back in the grass.

EDWARD AND ALPHONSE had two reasons for coming back to Dublith, a town they had not visited once since finishing their initial training.

First, they wanted to grow stronger.

Since leaving Resembool, the two had been engaged in a quest for information about the Philosopher's Stone. The Philosopher's Stone, spoken of only in rumors, was a magical tool for performing alchemy unfettered by the basic rules of equivalent exchange and the preservation of mass. Many were the people entranced by the limitless possibilities of the stone. Some of them were willing to hurt others for information and defend what little scraps of evidence they had with their lives. The Elric brothers had run into more than their share of scrapes, and recently, a few that they feared they might not walk away from. So they had come back once again to their old teacher Izumi in Dublith for special training.

Their second reason was to ask Izumi herself about the Philosopher's Stone. However, they soon found she had little interest in such things. So, while they endured their training in Dublith, they looked for other ways to learn more about the Philosopher's Stone.

"Ack, she hits hard . . ." Edward groaned, rubbing his sore jaw as he and Alphonse ran through the evening streets. Combat training had finished without either Edward or Alphonse landing one blow on their teacher. They had now moved on to the running portion of the day's activities. While they ran, they made a point of stopping to look through bookstores and antique shops and any other place that might hold clues.

Alphonse glanced over at Edward, who was busy cooling off his cheek with his automail right hand, and chuckled. "You have to remember to be more polite with her, Ed."

He joined his brother in every step of the training. Even though Alphonse could run for days without feeling the slightest bit of fatigue, it was Izumi's opinion that even if he couldn't train his body, the rigid regimen of exercise would train his spirit.

The two passed down a row of shops closing for the night until they were on the street leading to Curtis's Meats.

"I swear," Edward said, patting his arms and legs, "she doesn't know the meaning of restraint. I hurt all over." Tiny pebbles and sand still in the folds of his clothes clattered to the cobblestones below. After a full day of muscle training and being thrown this way and that, the two boys were covered with grime.

"Well, we did ask her to train us," Alphonse noted, wiping off his armor.

Edward grinned. "What were we thinking?" Squinting into the sun hanging low in the sky, he spat out a grain of sand stuck to his lip.

Since he had first trained with her, he felt that being near Izumi would not only strengthen his body, but his heart as well. She always stood straight, looking forward, not a crooked bone in her body. And when she faced you, she always did so with fairness in her eyes. Her fists were swift to fly at the slightest hint of impudence or an offhand remark, yet she was never really upset. She had this aura that made even the people standing near her seem more centered, more balanced.

"I just need to get stronger . . . so we can get our bodies back!" Edward declared.

Getting stronger and finding clues were not easy tasks. That's why he had time for neither exhaustion nor depression. "All right, it's last-spurt time! Race you to Curtis's, Al!"

"You're on!"

Lamps flickered on throughout Dublith in the growing dusk. Edward and Alphonse ran as fast as they could, feet pounding through pools of light spilling out of windows onto the cobblestones.

BY THE TIME Edward made it to Curtis's Meats, the shop had already closed for the day, and the smell of dinner drifted in the air. He opened the service door on the side of the building and went into the kitchen.

"I'm back!"

"Hey there, Edward," answered Sig, looking up from his beef stir-fry. Sig was a big man, with short black hair swept back over his head, a bristly beard, and rippling muscles under a white shirt that always made Edward think of a large, stubborn bear.

Next to him, Izumi stirred the contents of a large pot with a ladle. "Dinner soon, and it's quite a feast. Got to replenish those calories!"

Edward peered into the pot to see she was cooking his favorite: stew.

"All right!"

"Care for a taste?" Izumi smiled at his unmasked excitement and held up the ladle to his mouth. The stew was rich with vegetables and meat, perfect for a growing boy.

Though Izumi was a strict teacher, she wasn't unkind. Even after she learned that Edward and Alphonse had dabbled in human transmutation, even after they had left her once, she welcomed them back with affection.

Edward thanked her to himself while glancing around the kitchen.

"Hey, I can help. What should I do?"

"How about getting out plates and cups for everyone?"

"I'm on it!"

Edward picked up a stack of plates and carried them into the next room.

This room, with its round table and cabinet along the wall, was where they ate their meals and drank tea in the afternoons. It had a warm, homey feel, with flowers blooming in a small planter in the corner and books and the radio sitting on the shelves.

The radio was on, tuned to the news. Edward half listened to it as he set the table.

". . . identity of the suspect in the bombing of a military facility . . . took place in the middle of the night, an arrest was made at Central Station . . . military troops clashed with demonstrators on the northeast border . . . standoff since afternoon finally broke as . . . *fzzt fzzt fzzt* . . . chimeras thought to have escaped a private research laboratory . . . gone wild . . . several attacks . . . *zzzat zzzat zzzat* . . . *beep* . . . mobilized a small force . . . next in the new . . . *zzt zzt* . . . terrorist group claiming responsibility for an explosion near a munitions factory in the southwest . . . *vzza* . . . *vzza* . . . declared control . . . has called for a quick surrender . . ."

Edward frowned. The reception grew so bad it was hard to listen to.

Though Izumi was an alchemist, she believed that you should fix what you could with your hands, which meant that a lot of things that could have been fixed easily tended to lie around abandoned. The radio spluttered in and out, relating news about troop movements and military recruitment offers.

"They can recruit every able-bodied man and woman, and they still wouldn't have enough people to keep the peace," Izumi remarked. She had been listening to the radio through the open door to the kitchen. "When are they sending you to the front lines, Edward? You should quit that state alchemist's job before it's too late."

"Oh, I couldn't . . . Ha ha," Edward stammered, forcing an uneasy laugh.

State alchemists used their alchemy to serve the military state; many thought of them as the army's attack dogs. Izumi was of that opinion, and she never failed to give Edward a hard time about his job whenever they met. Lately, she skipped teasing him about it and simply told him to quit outright. Still, even though she was his teacher, he couldn't just give up on his duties like that. Nor could he really talk back.

Edward picked up the radio. "Let me fix this for you," he called toward the kitchen in an effort to change the subject.

"Oh, sure. Thanks," Izumi said, distracted by the arrival of Alphonse, who had finally made it back to the shop.

Edward breathed a sigh of relief and picked up the radio. He couldn't figure out whether a part of the radio was broken or whether there was a connection issue with the cord. He shook it a bit, and the reception got worse.

Edward had never been good with the detail work and was quick to give up. He could hear Alphonse, Izumi, and Sig chatting in the kitchen. A wall stood between them, keeping them from seeing what he was doing.

"Time for a little alchemy . . ." Edward said, softly putting his hands together, when a voice came from the kitchen.

"Oh, and Ed, I want you to fix it without using alchemy!"

". . . All right." Edward frowned and put the radio back down in the middle of the shelf.

Then he lifted his left hand, holding the fingers together rigid, like a blade, and took a deep breath.

"Hyah!"

He'd been hoping to knock it back into working order, but apparently he had dealt the radio the killing blow. There was a loud crunching noise, and the radio went perfectly silent.

"Huh? That's strange . . ." Edward shrugged just as a ladle came flying from the kitchen.

"You're the one who's strange!"

The ladle, thrown with expert control, caught Edward square in the back of his head.

"Ouch! Hey, it worked on my radio at home!" Edward protested, rubbing his head. "Yikes!" He shouted, catching the pot lid that flew after it. "It's your fault for buying such a cheap radio," he muttered quietly.

Not only had hitting it not helped, but the force of the blow had knocked four or five books off the shelf and onto the floor.

Edward started to pick them up, when he paused. ". . . Huh?"

Something tugged at the corner of his memory. Among the books lying on the floor was an album, opened to a page with several photos of Izumi and Sig. Edward squinted his eyes, focusing on one of the photos.

"Hey . . . !"

He sat down on the floor to get a closer look.

The photo showed Izumi and Sig surrounded by several adults and children, all smiling happily. It had been taken in some town. Edward could see a cobblestone street behind them and several houses.

Edward focused on the background. There was a bookstore, its glass door sitting open, and several books had been placed with the covers facing out the window.

If they had been just any books, he would have passed them over as part of the scenery. But one caught his eye.

"*The Evolution of the Body* . . . ?!"

He had heard that title before. Edward picked up the album, holding it so close his nose almost touched it, and stared. "That's it!"

"Al, *The Evolution of the Body!* It's here! It's right here in this picture!"

Together, the brothers had read practically every book that had even a remote chance of containing some clue to the secrets of human transmutation, yet still there were books they had never seen. Balerea Dell's *The Evolution of the Body* was one of them.

Balerea Dell was a rare breed, being both physician and alchemist. He had made the mending of the body his life's work, with a focus on the regenerative properties of alchemical treatments. The book had been published before the Elric brothers were born, but they had heard about it and the wealth of knowledge it contained.

The only problem was that *The Evolution of the Body* had been banned and pulled off the shelves.

There were several rumors as to the reason for the recall. Some said the regeneration of the body Dr. Dell talked about was a pack of lies. Others claimed that one of his rivals had instigated the recall to destroy the book and Dr. Dell's reputation. No one knew the truth.

Huge advances had been made in both medicine and alchemy since the book had been published. Much of the information it contained would likely be outdated or irrelevant. Yet the thought of seeing the very issue that they were researching from another person's perspective made the book's value priceless.

Edward wished he could reach in and grab it right out of the photo.

Alphonse looked at the photograph with astonishment. "So it really exists! I wonder when this photo was taken? It looks pretty old." He flipped it over to find a date written on the other side. Edward pieced together the faded numbers.

"Eighteen . . . ninety-seven? It's hard to make it out, but that's about when this book was published."

Chances were that it had already been recalled or sold. But just knowing that the book actually existed, that it wasn't an empty rumor after all, made Edward dream the impossible. They were clutching at straws as it was with their research. Sure, the chances were slim indeed that the book was still there, but could he really let it go without making absolutely sure?

"Where was this photo taken? Let's ask Izumi."

Edward stood and, as if on cue, Izumi and Sig came in from the kitchen, bearing plates of food. "Just leave the radio as it is, and take a seat. Some help you turned out to be . . ."

"Mrs. Curtis!" Edward said, grabbing a chair and bumping into the table in his excitement.

"Hey, you'll spill your stew!"

"Ouch . . . Sorry! Look, can you tell me where this was taken?!"

Izumi gave the boy a dubious look and took the album from his hands. "What's this all about? Which picture?"

"This one. Can you tell me what town this was taken in?" Edward asked, finally getting his breath under control.

"Where it was taken? Hmm, good question. It was quite some time ago . . ."

Izumi furrowed her brow and thought.

Sig leaned over to take a look at the picture. ". . . Isn't that Lambsear?" Lambsear was a larger town to the southeast. "That really takes me back. We spent some time walking around there, made some friends with the local kids. I think this is the picture we took when we said goodbye."

"Oh, yeah, heh, I'd completely forgotten about that." Izumi laughed and shook her head.

"Do you know anything about this bookshop you're standing in front of?"

"The bookshop? Oh, look at that." Izumi nodded and smiled. "I remember that place, sure. I think the owner's name was Egger. He sure had a lot of books. He was one of these real book freaks, had to read everything published. His house looked about to collapse from all the stacks of books. His family got mad at him, and eventually he had to start selling them. I heard he passed away about ten years back . . . Maybe one of his children or grandchildren is running it now." Izumi stared at the photograph, a wistful look in her eyes. "We were just married. I think I went in there looking for a cookbook so Sig here could make me something yummy."

Next to her Sig blushed and put a hand to his cheek. Izumi poked him in the stomach. "You were dashing back then, you know . . ."

"Back then . . . ?" Sig's face went from one of fond reminiscence to ire in the blink of an eye. "Hey! What about now?"

Slap! went Izumi's open hand on Sig's shoulder. She laughed.

Next to them, Edward and Alphonse were deep in discussion.

"If this guy liked books so much, maybe he kept a copy for himself when the recall came in."

"Maybe it's still there!"

"What's that? Are you two after some book? Why don't you go to the bookstore by the station? And don't you have access to that State Library, anyway, Ed?" Izumi asked. Apparently she and Sig had finished whispering sweet nothings to each other and she was paying attention to their conversation again.

"That would be fine for a normal book, but this one isn't normal." Edward showed the book pictured in the middle of the photograph to Izumi. "It's by Dr. Balerea Dell . . . Heard of him?"

"Balerea Dell? You mean *The Evolution of the Body* Balerea Dell?"

Suddenly, Izumi's expression grew hard. She lowered her eyes to the photograph again, then stared at the two brothers.

Just as Edward and Alphonse had once meddled in human transmutation, so too had Izumi practiced the forbidden art in the past. Balerea Dell was a name she knew well. "So what, you want to go and see if the book is still there?"

"We do. Would it be all right if we went to Lambsear tomorrow?"

Izumi looked at the photo for some time, then lifting her head, she shook it. "Not a chance."

"What?!"

"Why not?"

Edward and Alphonse jerked upright in response to this unexpected opposition.

When Izumi spoke, she was calm and cool. "Maybe you don't know this, but the author of this book, Dr. Dell, was thrown out of the academy. You can be sure that whatever is written in there will be none too reliable."

"Yes, but we might find something, a clue that will lead us to real information. We have to try!"

"And I say you don't. You may not officially be my students anymore, but I can't recommend this book. It would do more harm than good."

Edward and Alphonse pleaded, but Izumi remained adamant.

Regardless of why it had been banned, books like this one suffered from a bad reputation. And this book hadn't just been banned—it had been prohibited, recalled. They didn't even keep a copy in the State Library. Going after a book like that was going against the law. Izumi had always helped them gather information about human transmutation before, but something this risky gave her pause.

"Oh, well . . ." Edward said, dejectedly sitting back down in his chair. Alphonse slumped into his beside him.

"Now eat up. Your stew's getting cold."

Edward and Alphonse picked up their spoons, and with that, the discussion was over.

WHICH isn't to say they had given up.

As light gradually crept into the eastern sky, shadows moved on the second floor of the Curtis house, which stood that morning wrapped in silence.

"The map, change of clothes . . . Oh, wallet!"

In the small guest room, Edward was shoving things in his traveling trunk. Alphonse sat next to him, pen in hand, writing a letter.

"Um . . . Dear Izumi. We've gone to Lambsear. Please don't worry, we'll be back in two or three days. Sorry we can't help out at the shop . . . There, it's done."

"Good. The first train will be leaving soon. Let's go."

Edward put on his red coat, and opening the door carefully so as not to make a sound, he went downstairs.

He had considered telling Izumi they would be going to Lambsear. In the end, he decided it was better this way. She might get angry and try to stop them, or worse, ask to go with them.

The brothers knew how much she had done for them already. Sick as she was, she would stay up late at night writing letters to other alchemists, looking for information about the stone on their behalf. He didn't want to ask more of her than he already had.

They walked down the creaking stairs as quietly as possible and placed the letter on the shelf at the bottom.

"Sorry, Mrs. Curtis!"

"We'll be right back."

The two bowed their heads toward the room where Izumi and Sig still slept, then quietly opened the front door.

The dawn air was chilly, the street still dark. Edward quietly closed the door, and the two walked across the lawn and through the gate. They took one last look back at the house to make sure Izumi and Sig hadn't woken up.

"All right, let's do this!"

Then they started running, their footsteps echoing through the streets of the sleeping town.

As Edward ran, he waved his hands in front of his face. "This fog is unreal!" A heavy blanket covered the town, unusual for Dublith.

As it grew gradually lighter, the fog seemed to glow with a white light, appearing even thicker than before. They could see only a few feet ahead of them. It was like walking through smoke. Their pace gradually lessened.

"What's going on? I can't see a thing," Edward muttered.

Ahead of them, something moved.

"Huh . . . ?"

Alphonse noticed it too, and the boys stopped.

"You don't think it's Izumi, do you?"

"No way, the sun hasn't even risen yet."

The Curtises were early risers on account of their store, which is precisely why Edward and Alphonse had made a point of leaving before dawn.

The shadowy form in front of them came closer. It hunkered low to the ground, where the mist was thinner, and they could make out something like legs.

"Al!" Edward shouted, just as the thing leapt out of the mist toward them.

"Yikes!" Alphonse ducked, and it flew over his head, landing on the ground behind him. It was an animal, but no normal animal.

"What the heck?!"

The shadowy figure emerged from the mist, revealing two sharp eyes that seemed to burrow into Edward's heart and an open, toothy maw, dripping with saliva. The creature had a long tail and a coat of thick, black fur, making it look like a wolf. Except that Edward had never seen a wolf with six legs.

"A chimera!"

"What's a chimera doing here?!"

As they stood dumbfounded, two more chimeras emerged from the mist. They stood in a circle around the boys, growling low in their throats. Edward frowned. The chimeras looked ready to leap at any moment.

"I've got a bad feeling about this . . ."

"Hey, weren't they saying on the news that some chimeras had escaped from a research laboratory?"

"Yeah. The ones that were attacking people."

Edward had heard the news too. He just hadn't expected he and Alphonse would be the people.

"Let's hope they're not hungry."

As if in answer, the chimeras' growling increased in intensity.

"Al, there's a military police station office near by. Go tell them."

These chimeras had to be dealt with quickly before people started waking up, or there might be casualties.

"Roger. You be careful, Ed."

"You bet."

Alphonse ran off, and the chimeras twisted, following him with their necks. But it seemed that the armored Alphonse was less of a promising morsel than the boy of flesh and blood standing in front of them. As one, their eyes fixed on Edward.

The chimeras began to circle, scratching at the dirt beneath their claws.

"I warn you, I'm not very tasty." Edward sat down his trunk, and raised his arms to make a weapon with his alchemy. The chimeras howled as Edward clapped his hands together.

Just then, a voice in the mist shouted "Stop!"

Edward stopped, as did the chimeras.

Edward scanned his surroundings, looking for the source of the voice. He could see a shape in the gradually thinning mist. "Hey, you! These are chimeras! Run! You're in danger!" Edward took a step forward, but the shape disappeared. The chimeras turned and ran off in pursuit.

"H-hey!" Edward followed after them as best as he could, fearing that the chimeras had found a new victim. But they moved too quickly, and he soon lost sight of them. In his frustration, Edward dashed around, peering through the mist, but it seemed that both the person and the chimeras had vanished.

"What was that all about?"

The whole standoff had taken only a few minutes. The mist gradually grew lighter, revealing a quiet morning scene to Edward's untrusting eyes.

People would be waking up soon. A ray of light from the eastern sky lit up roofs of the town, floating in a sea of mist. Edward stood, getting his bearings, when he heard the faint sound of a train sliding along rails come from the direction of the station.

"Uh-oh!"

The sound snapped Edward back to reality. The first train of the morning would be leaving soon. That sound he heard was the sound of a train rolling out of the warehouse where the trains slept away the night.

"Ed!" Alphonse came running up with three military police officers behind him.

Their leader shouted out to Edward. "You there, where did the chimeras go?!"

"I think they ran out of town."

The officers frowned. "We need to tell the neighboring towns! Send in a bulletin to headquarters!"

The military police burst into action. Edward described a chimera to them as best he could, then turned to his brother.

"Al, we have to hurry. The train will be leaving soon!"

"Shouldn't we stay to help the police officers?"

"I'm betting that those chimeras are long gone. We should leave the investigation to them. Let's get going!"

"Right!"

The brothers took off at full speed. Soon they could see white steam rising from a locomotive engine, behind which stretched several passenger cars.

Edward ran into the station and made straight for the ticket booth.

"Two tickets please!" he shouted, reaching into his pocket for his wallet.

"For where, son?" the ticket seller asked.

"Uh . . ." Edward thought. He had momentarily forgotten where they were going in the morning's excitement.

". . . Lambsear," answered another voice from behind him.

Edward and Alphonse whirled around in astonishment, hoping beyond hope that the person who'd spoken was not who they thought it was.

It was.

"Mrs. Curtis!"

Izumi stood behind them, arms folded across her chest. "You two sure get up early."

Edward and Alphonse tried to think of something to say, but all thought stopped under that baleful gaze.

"Let me guess you didn't get up this early to get a head start on the day's jogging."

"Uh, well, actually . . ."

"Erm . . ."

Edward and Alphonse stood rooted to the spot, trembling. Almost casually, Izumi reached out her arms.

". . . Yeearg!"

The moment after Edward realized she had grabbed him by the arm, his world flipped upside down, and he smacked into the ground. While he was figuring out what had happened, he heard Alphonse shout from beside him, and his brother joined him on the ground.

"Idiots! Did you think I wouldn't know what you were up to?!"

The two boys were rolling and moaning on the ground as Izumi stood over them. Edward and Alphonse looked at each other, then sheepishly back up at Izumi.

"Would it kill you to take a person's advice every once in a while?"

Izumi glared at the boys, brushing back a lock of hair from her forehead with a sigh.

Edward and Alphonse held their breath, afraid of what might come next. This wasn't a first offense. They had gone against their teacher's wishes before.

"I'm sorr—" began Edward, when he was interrupted by a small, soft package landing on his head.

"It's a ways to Lambsear. You'll want some breakfast."

Edward took the package in his hand. It was a sandwich, wrapped in foil paper.

"You'll never get any taller if you don't eat right. And here, this is for you, Al. I stuck a memo inside with the address of the bookshop."

Izumi reached down to lend a hand to Alphonse as he got up off the ground and gave him a boy's comic book. It would give him something to do while Edward was eating breakfast.

The boys stood, at a loss for words. Izumi looked them over sternly, then her face broke into a smile for the first time.

"I knew you wouldn't listen if I just told you to stop. So go! And be careful."

She turned the two boys around and gave them a slap on the back.

Edward and Alphonse smiled.

"Thanks, Teach!"

"Thanks!"

Beyond the gate, the train whistle blew.

MEANWHILE, far away from Dublith at Eastern Command, Roy Mustang furrowed his brow at the telephone on his desk. Roy was the commanding officer at Eastern Command and a full-fledged state alchemist. The shock of black hair on his head and his jet black eyes gave him a boyish appearance, but the fact that he had attained the rank of colonel while still a young man was a testament to his sharp powers of perception and keen analytical mind.

"Ridiculous . . ."

Roy continued to glare at the phone, as if it would ring again and take back the orders he had just received.

The bright morning sun filled the officer's room, but it did nothing to lighten Roy's spirits. He stood and made for the ops room, where his subordinates had been working through the night.

Eastern Command was in charge of several bases scattered around the eastern part of the country. Hundreds of reports came in every day. The communications officer, sitting in front of a wireless transmitter, took down the reports from each region and passed them along to the responsible officer, who in turn gave the appropriate orders to be relayed back to the regional bases. These officers were under Roy's command, and it was his responsibility to keep them functioning. One never lacked for work when one was in charge of the entire eastern sector.

The early morning ops room was silent. Roy walked over and stood in front of the large desk reserved for him. He called out to the other officers still there from the evening before: First Lieutenant Riza Hawkeye, Second Lieutenant Jean Havoc, and Second Lieutenant Heymans Breda.

"You want us, sir?"

Even though she had worked through the night, Hawkeye stood straight and stern. She was a gifted officer, and Roy's second in command. She kept her blonde hair tightly bound behind her head, and somehow she always managed to seem crisp and ready for duty, no matter what the situation. Her track record was impressive too. Of all the officers at Eastern Command, she seemed the one to watch.

"Good morning, sir!" said Breda next to her. In contrast to Hawkeye, with her slim physique, Breda was a thickset man with a square face over a short neck and his hair closely shaven on the sides and back of his head. Breda was as rugged and hearty as they came, but he was no slouch in the smarts department. He never once lost at a game of chess and had a reputation throughout the base as a gifted thinker.

"Man, am I sleepy."

And then there was Havoc. Havoc could always be seen with an unlit cigarette dangling from the corner of his mouth, and he talked like he was laughing at some private joke. Though he was quite tall, he walked with a slouch and gave a distinctly mischievous impression. But when push came to shove, he was good at making swift, accurate decisions, and he always backed up Roy in a pinch.

Roy waited until the three were standing in front of him before he spoke again. "How many jobs are you all working on now? Having trouble with any of them?"

Breda responded first. "I'm working on three cases right now, including the resurgence in urban fighting from the other day, but I'll be finished with that soon."

"I'm doing the same thing he's doing," said Havoc.

"I have five ongoing investigations into terrorist activities, but I can't say they're giving me trouble . . . Has something come up?" Hawkeye asked.

Roy nodded. "I want you to delegate your current tasks to others. I've got a different assignment for you three."

"A different assignment, sir?"

"Just got a call in from Central. We have orders concerning those wild chimeras. They want it cleaned up in a week."

The incidents involving the chimeras had started several months ago, when a few of the strange creatures escaped from some research laboratory somewhere and began attacking people. They had been hiding out in mountains and forests, occasionally appearing to attack and then disappearing abruptly, frustrating all the military's attempts to control them.

All the chimeras sighted had two similarities: sharp fangs and a thirst for human blood. On occasion they would merely appear, wander about, and then disappear again, but every now and then, they would attack, and their victims inevitably wound up in the hospital with massive blood loss.

Though none of the victims so far had actually died, it was only a matter of time before one did.

Up until now, Central had left the containment of the chimeras to the regional offices, but civilian complaints had been mounting.

"We're supposed to catch these chimeras and find the person who set them loose. Their creations may not have taken any lives, but they've hurt several people and caused numerous disturbances, and someone has to take responsibility."

"A chimera hunt, huh? Sounds great," said Havoc.

Roy nodded with a sigh.

Chimeras were creatures remade from several unrelated species, blended together by alchemy. It was a difficult process, and much research remained to be done in the field, which meant that several alchemists were out there seeking to make a name for themselves by creating the strange beasts.

"There are several facilities within our borders researching chimeras. Some are military, others are biological laboratories run by individuals, and some alchemists are making their own chimeras on a very small scale . . . Apparently some laboratories strapped for cash have even sold their creations. In other words, they're too many possibilities to start narrowing down the suspects from the list. Nor do we even have a complete list . . . not that we can tell the public that."

"So the military, charged with protecting the state, had no oversight on the facilities making these dangerous chimeras—is that the picture?" Havoc asked with a wry smile.

Roy had been leaning on his desk. Now he stood straight. "These wild chimeras have been spotted in the southern and eastern parts of the country. On Central's orders, a team from Eastern Command and one from Southern Command will cooperate to solve this case quickly. We should hear from Southern about their progress soon. Let me know when they contact us. And I want all the information on the locations where the chimeras were spotted—pictures, witness accounts, anything you can find."

At Roy's command, the three went straight to work.

Hawkeye had one of her subordinates start gathering materials on the chimera sightings, then went over to the communications officer to await word from Southern.

"Who's going to lead the team from Eastern Command, sir?" Hawkeye asked, turning from the wireless transmitter.

Roy pointed at himself. "I will."

"You, Colonel?" Hawkeye asked, staring at Roy for a moment. Breda, busily sorting through maps to nail down where the chimeras had been spotted, stopped and looked up.

"You sure you want to tangle with those chimeras?" Havoc said, asking the question on all their minds. "I mean, you really think this is the time?"

Next to him, Breda nodded, agreeing.

"You have to admit, Colonel, they have a point," Hawkeye said, turning her clear brown eyes to Roy.

Roy knew all too well what they meant.

Barring emergencies, a commanding officer rarely went on frontline duty.

Catching some wild chimeras was tantamount to rounding up stray dogs. He could easily entrust the team's command to subordinates. What's more, Roy was scheduled to transfer from Eastern Command to Central the following week. He should have been spending that time preparing his successor and making other arrangements for the move to Central. Mountains of documents needed signing, secret materials needed proper filing. He didn't have time to bother with any chimeras.

"No, I intend to take command of this operation personally," Roy repeated.

"Well, if you say so, Colonel . . ."

"You know what needs to be done. Get to it," Roy said. After giving a few more directions, he returned to the officers' room.

Alone again, Roy sat at his desk and quietly opened the drawer. A single photograph sat inside.

"You'd probably be mad at me, wouldn't you? Tell me to choose my work. If only I had that luxury," Roy muttered as he softly closed the drawer. ◉

CHAPTER 2

THICKER THAN BLOOD

───────────────────────────────⊕

THE TRAIN EMERGED from a tunnel cut into the base of the mountain range, smoke streaming behind as it sped along the tracks.

"Hey, Ed, we're almost there!" Alphonse opened the window to better see the view.

Edward had been drifting off to sleep in the seat across from his brother. At the sound of his voice, Edward's eyes flickered open. He joined Alphonse, standing up and sticking his head out the window. A cool breeze blew against his cheek. "Feels nice!"

Edward took a deep breath. He had been expecting an oppressive heat this close to the desert, but the air was surprisingly pleasant. "Hey, the town's pretty big!" he shouted over the roar of the locomotive. "Look at that, Al, a river!"

"I guess that's why they call this place the last oasis!" Alphonse shouted back.

The train was now running along the mountainside. Down-slope, an embankment dropped to a wide, flowing river. Several houses stood on a gently rolling hill on the opposite side.

The sun there was hotter, it being well to the southeast of Dublith, but the wind hitting the mountains above and the large river worked to cool the air in Lambsear, making for a very temperate climate.

The river glittered in the sun, reflecting a wavelike pattern of light on the brothers' faces as they leaned out the window. The train, running parallel to the river, gradually began to slow, until they came to a stop at a station with a view of town streets.

Edward and Alphonse left the train with a crowd of other travelers and merchants, exiting the station and crossing the cobblestone street that ran before the gates. On the far side of the street stood a small wall, the other side of which dropped down to a rocky bank and the wide river running below. Turning back to look at the station, they could see the rails and several warehouses lined up against a backdrop of high, sun-drenched mountains.

It was a large town, yet it hadn't forgotten its natural sur-roundings—surely a last oasis here on the edge of the desert. After pausing to take in the scene, the two brothers got down to business.

"Okay, so now to find this Mr. Egger fellow's bookshop. Third Avenue, was it?"

Edward yawned deeply, stretched, and then pulled Izumi's memo from his pocket. "Looks like it goes First Avenue, Second Avenue, Third Avenue, down to Fifth, from north to south. So we need to go right to the middle."

Alphonse ran his hand across the map. He had spoken to the conductor while Edward was sleeping and learned that the station sat along First Avenue.

"Looks like we have to cross this river if we want to go any farther south. There's a bridge nearby."

According to the map, five bridges crossed the river. They headed for the one closest to the station. A small hill with an orchard rose on the other side of the river. Several houses lined the foot of the hill, also with fruit trees, each bearing an orange fruit neither Alphonse or Edward had ever seen before. This was the part about traveling they liked the most: seeing new things. Sometimes, they would buy strange fruits and other products they found at their destinations as gifts; other times, they would simply take stories home to tell to their friends.

They walked, soaking in the sights until they reached the bridge, where they came to a sudden stop.

A row of military police stood guarding the bridge. They were waving away any who tried to cross.

"This bridge is temporarily closed! Use another!"

"Hey, you there, get lost! Go home!"

Large signs deterring pedestrians were set on either edge of the bridge, and a low chain gate ran across the entrance.

"What, is the bridge broken?"

"It doesn't look like it . . ."

Edward walked closer, craning his neck to see. The bridge, made of wooden planks stretched over an iron framework, ran straight from the street on their side of the river to the raised wall on the opposite bank. Edward couldn't see anything that looked in need of repair.

One of the military police officers noticed the boys staring at the bridge and walked toward them. "Hey, you two!" he called from the other side of the gate. "What are you doing?"

Edward instinctively flinched at the man's haughty tone. "We're looking at the bridge. What of it?" he shot back, not bothering to be polite.

The officer's jaw tightened. "What did you say, boy?"

"Uh, uh, we were just wondering why the bridge was closed," Alphonse put in hastily. One look at his brother and the officer told him which way the winds were blowing, and he didn't want any trouble so soon after their arrival in this new town. Alphonse stepped forward to stand between the man and Edward.

"You heard about the chimera attacks?" the officer asked, his swagger somewhat diminished by Alphonse's considerable size.

"Have we ever," Edward chimed from over Alphonse's shoulder.

"Well, there's no telling when those wild chimeras will make their way to Lambsear. Brigadier General Bason lives on the other side of this bridge, and we have orders not to let so much as a rat near his residence."

"Bason . . . ?" Edward frowned.

Bason was a high-ranking officer at Southern Command. He was from a rich family, and rumors hinted that his money had more than a little to do with his current position. Edward had only ever seen him once, when they happened to pass by each other in the hall at Central. The man had pulled Edward aside and whispered, "Just because you're a state alchemist, don't think you'll make it anywhere in this army." It hadn't been the friendliest of meetings.

Beyond the bridge they could see a particularly large wall, and beyond that the roof of a mansion—the Bason residence.

"Isn't blocking off the entire bridge a little extreme?" Edward muttered, a little too loud.

"Ed!" Alphonse interjected, a little too late.

Apparently, the men working for the Brigadier General were as extreme as their master. The military police officer raised his eyebrows and stepped over the chain toward them. "Who are you, anyway? Travelers? Why did you come here?! I warn you, if you've got any plans against the Brigadier General . . ."

Edward swallowed. They couldn't exactly tell him they had come here to buy a banned book. Without a word, he turned and ran.

"Ed? Ed! Wait up!" Alphonse rushed after his quick-as-ever brother.

Running as fast as he could, Alphonse caught up. The officer was hot on their heels.

"Try to show a little more self-control, Ed!"

"Did you see that guy's attitude?"

"Yeah, but still . . ." Unlike his brother, Alphonse believed that fights were best avoided. "Why do you always have to stand out like that, anyway?"

Common sense would dictate that the giant, hulking suit of armor that was Alphonse would raise more eyebrows than his brother, but it was always Edward who seemed to stir up the crowds. Maybe his brother liked to take action, to stir things up, or maybe something else about him grabbed people's attention.

"What?" Edward asked breathlessly as he ran. "You think I'm too short to stand out, is that it?"

"That's not what I said. It's just—"

"I know what you were thinking, Al!"

While they argued, the brothers had run in a loop, circling back toward the station in order to shake their pursuer. Reaching the waist-high wall that dropped down to the river, Edward grabbed onto it with his hands and jumped over.

"Wait!" Alphonse shouted. "There might be someone on the . . ."

It was too late.

"Yipes!"

"Eeeek!"

From the riverbank below came Edward's surprised shout, followed quickly by a tiny scream.

". . . other side," Alphonse finished, shaking his head. He ran to the wall and looked down. At the bottom of the six-foot drop, Edward and a small child sat in the rocky grass of the riverbank. An overturned cardboard box lay in the grass by their side.

"Are you okay?!" Alphonse shouted, quickly lowering himself down the wall to kneel by the child.

It didn't look like Edward had fallen on him, rather that the boy had been so surprised to see Edward drop out of the sky he had tripped and stumbled. The boy wiped the sand off his hands and looked up.

"Ah . . . !"

Edward and Alphonse stood, mouths gaping open.

The boy could have been anywhere from six to eight years old. His light-colored hair was soft and seemed to float in the breeze. Even though it was a warm day, he wore a long-sleeve shirt and trousers that covered his ankles. The hands that emerged from the cuffs of his sleeves and the toes that poked through his sandals were brown. His eyes when he looked up at Edward and Alphonse shone bright red.

"An Ishvalan . . . !" Edward whispered.

The boy heard him and made a sour face.

The Ishvalan people lived in the southeastern reaches of the country of Amestris. There had been several clashes over differences in religion and other issues between the Ishvalans and the government of Amestris, culminating in a civil war thirteen years ago when a member of the Amestris military mistakenly shot an Ishvalan child. After five years of fighting, a large number of state alchemists were sent in, and in the resulting conflict, most of the Ishvalans were exterminated.

Since then, Amestrians and Ishvalans avoided each other, the former burdened with guilt over the massacre that had taken place with their blessing, and the latter having lost so many of their friends and kin. The Ishvalans who remained roamed far and wide to put as much distance between themselves and their sorrowful past as they could.

An uncomfortable silence lingered for a few moments.

The boy broke the awkward silence. "Good day," he said, his face breaking into a smile. His voice was bright and pleasant.

The boy's smile came as a great relief to Edward and Alphonse, who had been unsure whether they should apologize or just leave silently before they offended the boy any further.

"Oh, uh, good day to you!" Edward stammered.

"You must have been in a hurry!"

"I guess you could say that," Edward said, scratching his head and looking up at the wall. There was no sign of any military police anywhere. He turned back to the boy. "Look, I'm real sorry for scaring you like that. You sure you're okay?"

"I'm fine."

"Ed, you really have to learn to look before you leap," Alphonse said, shaking his head.

Edward reached toward the overturned box lying on the riverbank. One of the sides had come loose when the cardboard box fell.

"Sorry about that. I'll fix it right away." Edward went to pick it up, but the boy shook his head.

"No, I dropped it in a puddle on my way down here. It wasn't your fault."

"Still, you can't exactly carry it like that," Edward said, crouching before the boy. A pile of books for children lay scattered around. The slightly soggy cardboard box couldn't possibly hold them now.

Edward raised his hand, thinking to strengthen it with a little alchemy, but when he caught sight of the boy's red eyes on his hands, he quickly lowered them.

"Wait just a second," Edward said, looking down the riverbank. Junk had drifted along the river before washing up here and there along the bank. He spotted a coil of old rope among the garbage. Edward retrieved it and began reinforcing the box.

To most Ishvalans, alchemy was an object of fear and hate. Even though the boy was too young to remember the massacre, he had surely heard stories. Edward carefully fixed the box by hand, while Alphonse helped by picking up the books.

"There, all better!"

Bound by rope, the box was in working order again. Edward had even fashioned two loops on the top to use as a handle.

"Hey, thanks!" the boy said with a grin. Edward and Alphonse quickly placed the scattered books inside the box.

"What are these, picture books?"

Edward picked one up and flipped through the pages. In it were colorful scenes of animals eating at a table and holding hands.

"Yeah. I was lending them to a friend of mine down there." The boy pointed down the river to a small shack on the riverbank. Edward noticed several other shacks like it lined up along the river, below the level of the streets.

"That must be where the Ishvalans live," Alphonse whispered.

Edward nodded. "Good bet."

Robbed of a home to call their own, the Ishvalans had settled in the margins of other cities and the wilds along the borderlands, living in tight-knit groups huddled together for security. They were likely a common sight here in Lambsear, it being so close to Ishval, a region entirely abandoned since the war.

Alphonse carefully wiped the grime off the book and handed it to the boy. "There you go. That's quite a lot of books you have there."

"Of course, I live at a bookshop. Egger's Books, down on Third Avenue."

"What?!"

"Egger's Books?!"

Edward glanced at the books again and for the first time noticed a small sticker attached to the cover of one that read Egger's Books in small block letters.

"You must really like books!" the boy said, unsure how to read their reaction.

"Actually we're here in town looking for one . . ."

"Well, I'll take you to the shop!"

The two stared, amazed by the coincidence, but the boy mistook their amazement for suspicion.

" . . . I mean, if you want me to." The boy frowned. It was the face of someone who knew there were people in the world who wouldn't care to be seen walking with an Ishvalan out in the open.

"No, no, that'd be great!" Alphonse said, waving his hands. "We were just surprised at our luck."

The two stood from where they had been crouching by the river. "Please? Take us to your bookstore. My name's Edward. This is my brother, Alphonse."

"I'm Kip! Nice to meet you."

Edward offered a hand, which Kip took in his own and shook firmly. The boy's smile held not a trace of his people's tragic history.

KIP'S HOUSE stood at the top of a steep, winding road.

The house had white walls, a red roof, and double doors made out of glass, next to which hung a sign that read "BOOKS." The yellow and green paint of the sign had faded from years of exposure to the weather.

There was a private entrance on the side, with a small postbox standing next to it. Deep green vines had grown across the post, the doors, and the white walls of the shop, which balanced the other colors nicely. It was a large building, probably because it served as both a bookstore and a house, but not so large that it shadowed its neighbors to either side. If not for the sign, they might have mistaken it for just another residence.

Kip walked up to the glass doors and gave them a push, but they seemed to be closed. "Huh, maybe nobody's home. Hang on a second!" The boy ran around to the side door and darted inside.

Left on the street in front of the shop, Alphonse and Edward set down Kip's books and peered through the glass doors at the shop's interior.

"Well, looks like they're still in business!"

"Yeah . . ." Edward grumbled and looked up at the shop. The owner of the shop when Izumi had been here was probably Kip's grandfather, or even great grandfather. "I wonder how much they'll go out of their way to help a couple of Amestrians?"

"I hadn't thought of that . . ."

While they stood pondering their options, they heard Kip shout from inside.

"We've got customers! Hurry, hurry!"

Edward and Alphonse straightened themselves and looked over to the doors.

With a cheerful ringing of tiny bells, the glass doors opened. The person who stepped out was a slender woman of about thirty, an Amestrian. "I'm sorry, I meant to come right back to the shop but got held up," she told them. She smiled a gentle smile framed by wavy shoulder-length brown hair. Keeping her pretty blue eyes turned toward Edward and Alphonse, she opened the doors and used her toes to push a small rock in front of each to keep them from blowing shut.

"Please, come in."

"Hey, Mom. Edward and Alphonse here fixed my box for me!"

She's his mother?

"Did they? Well, hello. I'm Shelley. Thanks for helping my boy out." She turned back to Kip. "Kip, you go wash up. You've been running down by the river again, haven't you?"

"Yeah, Mom," he replied, and ran through a green door in the back.

Once his footsteps had faded entirely, Shelley turned back to the boys. "You must be surprised, I know. That boy . . . His parents went missing in the civil war. I'm taking care of him until they're found again."

"That's very kind of you," Alphonse told her.

Judging from Kip's age, he must have been separated from his parents right after being born. It was hard to imagine an innocent boy with such a bright smile could have such a dark past. After a moment, however, they remembered their reason for coming to the shop in the first place.

"Actually, we had heard of your bookstore—or rather, of a person who liked books, named Mr. Egger, who lived here?"

"Yes, my father-in-law. He passed away some time ago. He left the store to my husband."

"We're looking for a particular book. I was wondering if we could take a look around?"

Edward wanted to avoid dropping Balerea Dell's name if at all possible. He didn't want to raise suspicions, and mentioning they wanted a banned book might make Shelley start to worry about these two strangers she was letting into her shop.

"Certainly, of course. Have a look around," Shelley said with a smile, showing the two in. "The books aren't organized by genre, so it's a bit of a maze . . ."

"No problem at all. We'll just browse a bit. Right, Ed?"

"Right."

The brothers stepped inside the store.

"Wow, look at that!"

The middle of the store had a high ceiling, stretching at least another story above them. Shelves packed with books lined the walls. A small stair led up from the ground floor to a narrow walkway that circled the room above their heads, wide enough for a single person to walk around and look at the books near the tops of the massive shelves. To the right, a trapdoor in the floor sat open, revealing a staircase that led down to more shelves in the cellar below.

The bookshelves not only lined the walls but also stood in tight rows throughout the bookstore, and wherever an empty spot on the floor might have been, a free-standing stack of thick volumes stood piled instead. It was an oppressive quantity of books for one independent bookseller.

"Are all the books your father-in-law collected here?" Edward asked, wondering if he might have kept rare books with more value in some personal stash.

"Yes, for the most part," Shelley answered. "There are some picture books in my husband's study. Were you looking for a picture book?"

"No."

"Then, if we have it, it's out here. I'm sorry I can't say for certain with my husband out. If you like I can show you the study later. Take all the time you like."

She told them to call her if they needed anything and then disappeared into the back of the shop.

Edward and Alphonse stood in the center of the bookshop, staring at the shelves. It would take forever to search them all.

"It might have gotten sold or been recalled . . ."

"Well, we might as well get searching!"

Edward took off his coat and climbed the narrow staircase to the second-floor walkway. Hanging his coat on the railing, he started scanning titles on the books' spines, pulling out anything that looked suspicious.

"Look, a government history! First edition!"

"Hey, Ed! There's some books from the eastern kingdom here too!" Alphonse called from the stairs behind him. He had pulled a weighty tome off a shelf and held it cradled in his arms.

"Let's see . . . We have a cookbook, a book about insects . . . Hey, I've been looking for a book on metallurgy for a while!"

The two went over each book, spine by spine, checking the titles. Only a true book aficionado could have amassed such a varied collection. Most of the books they had never seen or even heard of. Yet finding all these rare books here meant the chances looked good that Balerea Dell's book was here too.

Hopes springing anew, they pored over the books in a daze.

When the back door opened again and Kip's face peered out, they had no idea how much time might have passed.

"Hey, Edward and Alphonse!"

"Hey there, Kip."

"Did you find your book?"

Kip had changed. He was wearing a short-sleeve shirt. He pulled a match out of his pocket and started lighting lamps around the store.

"Whoa! It's that late already?"

For the first time, Edward realized that dusk had fallen outside, and the inside of the bookshop had been growing quite dark.

He could have sworn only an hour had passed, but it was easy to forget time when you were so focused on a task. Alphonse, too, had completely lost track of time, and he hurriedly rushed to put back some of the books he had scattered around in his search.

"Better clean these up before they close for the night. Sorry for making such a mess."

"Don't worry about it," Kip said with a smile, then asked if they wanted some apple juice. "It's pretty hot in here."

Though a breeze was blowing in through the open doors, the air up along the walkway was stale and muggy. Edward was drenched in sweat. He went back down to the ground floor, accepted a glass and drank it in one gulp. Alphonse politely declined, so Edward drank his down too before stepping outside.

"Wow, it's practically night."

Outside, the evening wind tugged gently at his shirt collar. The streetlamps lit the cobblestones, and the silhouette of the mountain looking over the town was outlined in stars.

After cooling off, Edward went to step back inside when he noticed a row of picture books lined up in front of the "BOOKS" sign. Kip had probably put them there to dry after their spill in the puddle.

"Aren't these picture books out there for sale?" Edward asked, going back inside.

Kip shook his head. "Luon says not to sell the picture books. Instead, he loans them out so everyone can read them. That's why he keeps them all in his study."

"Luon?"

"He's the one taking care of me until my real parents are found," Kit said simply.

THE TIES THAT BIND

Luon must be Shelley's husband, the owner of the book-shop, Edward reasoned.

"He's really tall and really handsome. He gives me rides on his shoulders all the time! He's really good with his hands too. He makes me boxes for my scissors and stuff. He also likes to smoke his pipe, and I get to light it for him! See?"

Kip pulled a small matchbox out of his pocket. The back was white with a small picture of three people holding hands. "I asked him to draw me a picture once, and this is what he drew. He did one on all my other matchboxes too. This one we drew together." Kip went on about Luon until it was clear to Edward that the boy had truly accepted the man as his father for all intents and purposes.

"When he goes out to buy books for the shop, he always brings back a bunch of picture books for me. He lets me take them to my Ishvalan friends."

Edward and Alphonse nodded, impressed. This was some-body clearly doing his part to help the displaced refugees living in the city.

"Sounds like a nice guy."

"Is Luon out buying books now?"

"Yeah. He says all our books here are too specialized, so he's slowly replacing them with books that normal people want to read. He goes on buying trips all over the place."

Edward grinned, understanding. He had spent enough time in the bookshop to see that it was true. The books here dealt with every subject under the sun, and Edward had trouble imagining anyone but a true specialist wanting to buy any of them.

Of course, that very fact meant they had a chance at finding their book here.

Still, Edward shook his head. "There's no way we'll finish this today."

Even reading only the titles alone, they still had a lot of books left to check. They would have to come back tomorrow.

"I guess that's about it for today. I'm hungry anyway. Maybe you could tell us where we can find a restaurant and an inn?"

"An inn? Huh? You're leaving?"

The back door opened behind the boy and Sherry emerged. "Well? How did it go? Did you find your book?"

"Hey, Mom!" Kip ran straight back to her and grabbed onto her legs. "Mom, Edward and Alphonse are looking for an inn."

"Oh?" Shelley smiled and patted Kip on the head. "Why don't you stay with us?" she asked the brothers. "As you can see, we have quite a few books for you to look through. If you stayed here, you wouldn't have to worry about the time."

"But we couldn't—" Alphonse began.

"Haven't you heard about the wild chimeras? They haven't shown up in Lambsear yet, but it's still not safe to go out after dark."

Edward and Alphonse knew the threat of the chimeras all too well, having just run into them that morning, and the thought of being able to spend as much time as they wanted to looking through the books was appealing. Still, it felt wrong to impose when they weren't even sure they were going to buy anything.

Edward and Alphonse hesitated, but Kip broke away from Shelley and ran up to Edward, tugging on his sleeve. "Come on, it will be fun. We can talk and stuff. And Mom's a great cook. Aren't you, Mom? You can eat with us!"

As if on cue, Edward's stomach made a loud growling noise.

Alphonse, Kip, and Shelley burst out laughing.

"That sounds like an empty tummy."

"That *was* pretty loud, Edward!" Kip said giggling.

The sound of laughter filled the nighttime bookshop.

"The stomach has spoken, Ed. Shall we stay?" Alphonse asked.

"Why not. Thank you!" said Edward, joining in the laughter.

THE NEXT MORNING, Edward woke to a delicious smell wafting up from downstairs.

He checked the clock hanging on the wall. Seven. He had meant to wake up at six, but had stayed up too late the night before, searching through stacks of books.

He was alone in the room. Alphonse must have already gone down.

Getting out of bed, he opened the window and the pleasant morning breeze blew the sleepy fog out of his head. Beneath the second floor guestroom stood trees laden with fruit and flowers of all colors swaying gently in the sunlight.

The bookshop was across a small garden from the building where Edward had spent the night. Luon had told Shelley once that his father brought so many books into the house, they had to build a whole new house just to get some living space back.

"Maybe I'll check out the books in the cellar today . . ."

Edward washed up, got dressed, and went downstairs.

He peeked into the kitchen to find Shelley in a light green apron frying an egg. Kip was pulling plates out of a cupboard.

"Good morning," Edward said, squinting his eyes in the bright sunlit kitchen. The two looked in his direction.

"Hey ya, Edward!"

"Good morning. Did you sleep well? We're just making breakfast. Have a seat."

"Oh, thanks," said Edward, sitting down a little uneasily. He felt bad waking up last and doing nothing to help, but then again, he wasn't a very good cook anyhow.

"Alphonse is out picking some vegetables for us," Kip told him as he set the table. Edward looked out a small window with a planter hanging on the sill, and saw Alphonse on his knees in the garden, busily pulling up carrots.

"The coffee's ready, if you want some," said Shelley, never taking her eyes off the frying pan. Kip walked over to the coffee pot. "I'll get it, Mom."

"You sure?"

"Yeah, I can do it without spilling any now."

The boy picked up the coffee pot from the cooking table and carefully poured the steaming coffee into a mug. Carrying the mug in both hands so as not to spill a drop, he brought it to Edward. Then, he went over to stand on a painted, light blue box that sat beneath the sink. Even standing on the box, the sink looked high for him. Not seeming to care, he picked up some fruit from beside the sink. "Hey, Mom, can I squeeze these?"

"Sure, if you think you can do it."

"Watch me!"

Kip carefully washed the fruit, then going over to the cupboard and standing on his tiptoes, he pulled down a glass juicer. Standing on a chair, he squeezed each of the fruits as hard as he could. A fresh, citrusy scent filled the kitchen.

"Here you go, Edward." Kip set a glass down in front of Edward. It was brimming with fresh juice that sparkled in the sunlight streaming in through the windows.

"That was some good squeezing there. It looks delicious!" Edward patted the boy on the head and Kip grinned.

"Let me know if you want more. I can make as much as you can drink!"

"I dunno, I can drink a lot!" Edward said, smiling back.

"Hey, Mom," Kip said. "I'm going to help Alphonse. Oh, and I still have to sweep up in front of the shop!" The boy opened the door to the garden and ran outside.

The door closed behind him with a slam, and Shelley smiled. "I'm sorry. He's so restless in the morning."

"Oh, not at all," Edward replied. "It's great he helps out."

The night before, Kip had helped Shelley with dinner while he talked to Edward and Alphonse. He always seemed willing to give Shelley a hand.

While he waited for breakfast, Edward sipped his coffee and looked over at the photographs stuck on the wall.

He saw a picture of Kip, not even one year old, sleeping. There he was again, a little larger now, clinging to Shelley's leg. And another, this one with him laughing and reading a picture book. The Eggers were clearly Kip's mom and dad, even though they shared not a drop of common blood.

"I love all these pictures of Kip."

"I'm glad to hear you say that," Shelley said. "My husband takes as many as he can. He says it will be a good record of the boy's growth to show his parents when we find them."

Coffee cup in hand, Edward stood and walked over to the wall.

Below the photos was a shelf with a phone. Next to it hung one more photo, this one in a small frame, set apart from the rest. It wasn't part of the official record of Kip's growth.

The photo showed a slender man standing with one arm around Shelley and Kip in the other. His hair had been swept casually to the side of his forehead, and he and Shelley were smiling. The picture had been taken when the sun was low in the sky, in the cool of the evening.

"Is this Luon here?" Edward asked, looking back over his shoulder.

Shelley nodded, sliding an egg off the frying pan and onto the plate. "That's him." Shelley put some vegetables next to the egg, then went over to look at the photo with Edward.

"We took that two years ago. Actually, this is the only picture of the three of us together. I'd like to take another when he comes back."

"He's out buying books, right? He must be very busy."

"I don't know much about the business, actually, but I know he travels all over the place. He spends a little time looking for Kip's parents while he's gone, so it all works out well."

"Do you have any idea where they might be?"

"My husband knew them, actually. They entrusted him with Kip during the civil war and took refuge, although he never knew where. That's what I heard."

Edward glanced back at the photos hanging on the wall. It was easy to see the boy's growth from the progression of images. Luon would want to show his friends when they found them again.

"He must not come home often . . ."

"Not very. Lately, he makes it back about once every two months. Sometimes, I think he's more of a traveler than a bookseller. Though he does call often to tell me where he is, so I don't have to worry too much. Every time he comes home, he promises he'll find Kip's parents on the next trip. It's sort of a habit of his." Shelley smiled, then pointed to the table. "Go eat up, now."

"Thanks, gladly!"

Back on the table, Edward's plate was piled high with toast, eggs, vegetables, and fruit. He had managed to explain during dinner the night before that Alphonse simply didn't eat much, so she had made food only for one.

"Hey, Mom! Can I give one of the tomatoes that fell to the birds?" Kip called in from outside.

"Go ahead. Make sure to cut it into little bits for them!"

"Hey, where're the garden shears?"

Shelley seemed reluctant to get up from the table with Edward still eating. He waved toward the door, his mouth filled with toast.

"Excuse me," Shelley said, then got up and went out into the garden.

Alone at the table, Edward worked on his egg and thought about family. His own mother, Trisha, had been very smart. Edward and Alphonse had loved her and always helped around the house. Seeing Kip with his mother reminded Edward of how it had been for them. Things were different when it came to their fathers. Kip's came home at least once in a while, and it was clear the boy felt much gratitude and respect toward him. Edward and Alphonse's father had left and never returned.

Edward looked back at the photo.

Luon, Kip, and Shelley, smiling.

There, in the frame that hung by the phone, they were a family.

FWUMP.

The cloud from a tremendous explosion rose into the sky over a town on the border between the east and south.

"I told them not to use all those guns!"

Roy glared into the distance at the smoke rising from the munitions warehouse, shielding his eyes from fragments of plaster that fell from the walls with the shock of the blast. He frowned.

"Colonel!" a voice shouted. It was Hawkeye. "The plan was a failure," she said, saluting.

Roy sighed and pointed out the window. "I figured."

A steady wind blew the column of smoke across a clear blue sky.

After hearing reports of the wild chimeras appearing in a nearby town, Roy's team had quickly set up shop, borrowing an arms manufacturer's facility to set a trap for the creatures.

However, the leader of the team from Southern wasn't doing his job. He'd ended up only slowing them down . . . and infuriating Roy in the process.

Hawkeye opened a file. "We received a report from Master Sergeant Fuery just now. He says they've checked into all the facilities in the country capable of producing chimeras, but none report any escapes. Not surprisingly, they all deny connection with the incident. Also, Warrant Officer Falman says that they tried to capture one of the wild chimeras with a trap, but the bait didn't seem to be working. They used meat. Beef, it sounds like."

"That's because our friends have a taste for blood."

Havoc turned where he was standing a distance away from them. He had been in charge of the fire team who put out the blaze over at the munitions warehouse. If he was here, that meant the fire was under control.

Roy and Hawkeye started walking, fragments from the blast crunching under their feet. The air around the munitions warehouse smelled of smoke and burning plastic. The larger fires had been put out, but stacks of equipment here and there still smoldered. Soldiers ran back and forth, carrying buckets of water.

The roof and one of the walls had blown clear off the building, leaving only a blackened steel frame behind. Havoc looked dejected.

"Good work," Roy called out to him.

He turned, a crooked smile on his soot-blackened face. "Hot work."

"Any deaths or injuries?"

"Two soldiers got hit by shrapnel; they're off to the hospital. Think they'll make it, though. Oh, and one civilian. There was a blockade on the road, but some idiot soldier let him through, and he ran afoul of the chimeras."

"That's not good."

It would be Roy's responsibility if any civilians were attacked by the chimeras while the area was under his control. Roy furrowed his brow.

"Actually, it wasn't the chimeras that got him," Havoc explained, unconcerned. "Just as they were about to leap, an old building weakened by the blast next to the guy collapsed, blocking off the street. The civilian was so frightened he tripped and skinned his knee. Lucky, eh? Incidentally, Southern was in charge of that blockade."

"If that's luck, I'll pass."

"Better some luck than none." Shaking ash out of his blonde hair, Havoc continued his report. "Four chimeras were spotted. One of them ran out through a waterway. All of them matched the descriptions of the ones we've heard about in the reports so far: humongous wolves, ungainly fellows, with six legs each and fangs as sharp as knives. We had them surrounded, that part went well . . . but our backup from Southern was a bunch of fresh soldiers with no combat experience."

"They saw the chimeras and got scared," Roy said, imagining what had happened. He slapped himself on the forehead.

"Actually, they were so frightened that they . . ." Havoc held his fingers into a pistol shape and made a shooting motion.

"And set off a stack of ammunition sitting in a corner of the warehouse. I question the judgment of whoever sent a bunch of recruits to deal with such a sensitive issue. I'm just glad there were no casualties."

"The guy who's in charge of the Southern team, apparently he's famous for making mistakes. Kind of have to wonder why they sent them in the first place."

"I wonder," Roy said, scratching his chin. "I heard Brigadier General Bason nominated him to lead the mission . . ."

Havoc's mouth gaped open.

Bason was a big man at Southern Command, and one of Roy's more famous rivals. He would have known that Roy was leading the team from Eastern. So this was his way of throwing a monkey wrench in the plans.

"Well, that sucks, sir."

"Yes. Yes, it does," Roy agreed, walking over to stand by the waterway that ran next to the shattered munitions warehouse. The waterway was a trench that ran through the manufacturing park. For most of its length, wooden boards covered its span, but several had been blown off in the blast, leaving the trench exposed in one spot. It had been constructed to drain off excess water during heavy rains so that the warehouses would stay dry, and it was rather deep.

"So one of them got away through this trench?"

"Yes, sir. Probably through that section there where the boards were ripped up . . ."

Havoc took Roy over to the trench and lifted a square metal latch on the boards. Cool air came wafting up from the hole. Apparently water that came down through the trench was diverted into a full-fledged underground sewer here.

Roy looked into the hole. A ladder extended down from the rim, and light coming from somewhere glittered on the water below.

"Has anyone been down here since the chimeras escaped?"

"No. I know because I was standing on guard here the whole time."

"Well done."

Roy examined the ladder for any trace of passage carefully. Havoc was probably telling the truth about standing guard. He could see cigarette ashes on the ground nearby, and a faint smell of tobacco lingered in the air.

"Going to go down?" Hawkeye asked.

Roy nodded, taking off his jacket and handing it to Breda.

"Second Lieutenant Breda. Keep watch here and make sure no one else comes." Then Roy, Hawkeye, and Havoc climbed down the ladder.

At the bottom, they found themselves in a wide tunnel. The roof curved in a half cylinder, and the water ran along the floor. It hadn't rained much recently, so the flow barely covered the width of the sewer.

Taking care not to slip, Roy and the others gingerly stepped down into the water and took a look around.

The sewer seemed to stretch beneath the entire town. Here and there, the roof panels gave way to iron grates, through which slipped enough dim light for them to see by.

"Here's a map of the waterway, sir."

Hawkeye handed Roy a chart showing the paths the waterway took through town. A little farther ahead, it intersected with another tunnel going perpendicular, and each of these branches divided further into other tunnels.

"Looks like a real maze," Roy said, checking the map as they moved down the tunnel. Soon they came to an intersection.

"There's supposed to be a tunnel going this way on the map," Roy noted, pointing at a blank wall.

"Sewage is a very important part of town life," Havoc explained, going into lecture mode. "Apparently, a few years back, there was a big civilian movement in town to have new waterways made. Some of the old tunnels were repaired, others were sealed off. This must be one of them."

"You're probably right. Still, I don't know how we're going to find the chimeras down in this mess." Roy trudged through the shallow water, thinking. "If the chimeras used the waterway to escape, they might have used it to get here in the first place."

"You mean, they might have used the waterways to move unseen through the town, until they found a place large enough to hide where they could attack from?"

"Then we're kind of at a disadvantage, if they know the place and we don't. There are a lot of tunnels down here," Havoc said, walking behind Roy and Hawkeye. "Pretty smart for dumb animals, huh?"

He moved slowly, checking for signs of the chimeras' passage, only looking away from the wall when he realized that neither Roy or Hawkeye had said anything for a while.

The two were standing in the water, thinking.

"What's up?"

Roy looked back at Havoc. "Maybe they're not dumb animals."

"Huh?"

"What do we know about the chimeras? They've escaped from some laboratory and gone feral, and now they're hungry and attacking people. But what if we're wrong?"

"Wrong?" Hawkeye asked.

"What if they didn't escape from a laboratory? What if they were sent out for some purpose?"

The three fell silent.

The chimeras were attacking people, draining their blood. But what if they weren't doing it because they were hungry? What if someone had sent them out to take blood and collect it?

Roy looked up. "But that would mean . . ." Roy sloshed up to the section of wall where, on the map, there was supposed to be another tunnel. First, he patted the wall with the palm of one hand, then lightly knocked. Then Roy gave the wall a powerful kick with his foot.

"Hey!" Havoc turned in surprise.

With a great rumbling noise, the wall collapsed. After the dust had cleared, the old waterway was revealed. Roy bent down to remove the pieces of the wall that had fallen into the water. The fist-sized chunks of plaster crumbled easily in his hand.

"This wall was put here to prevent people from following the chimeras."

That would prove the attacks were intentional.

"Somebody's guiding them. And they don't want the army to find out. They made this wall weak, so it would crumble before too long . . . Wouldn't want the waterways clogging up and raising suspicion. And whoever it is, they're clearly an alchemist."

"Judging from the frequency of attacks," Hawkeye said, "the chimeras' controller requires fresh blood. If research continues while the chimeras are on the prowl, then we're dealing with at least two people: one to stay in the laboratory, and the other one to come out on the hunt."

"The chimeras were first spotted four months ago . . . and they may have started before then, and we just didn't know about it."

"That's a lot of blood," Havoc said. "Why would anyone need so much?"

"Not something I really want to think about," Roy said with distaste, turning back toward the tunnel they had followed to get here. "Still, this lets us narrow down the kind of laboratory we're looking for. On to the next phase!"

When they climbed back up the ladder, Breda was waiting for them at the top.

"Hello again, sir. Did you find anything?"

Roy nodded. "Lots. We have Havoc to thank for tracking a chimera down here."

"I'll expect special compensation, of course," Havoc interjected.

"And I'll consider it, but first we need to get that officer from Southern back to his base and out of our hair. And as for the next phase . . . " Roy walked while he spoke. He began putting his jacket back on when he stopped to wrinkle his nose at a trail of smoke drifting by.

He looked up to see Havoc bumming a cigarette off Breda, who lit it for him.

"Second Lieutenant Havoc."

"Yes, sir?"

"Did I just see you bum a cigarette and a light off Second Lieutenant Breda?"

"Well, I couldn't exactly smoke by the munitions warehouse. And my lighter was full, so I gave it to him before I left. Of course, now that everything that's flammable is already on fire, it's not a problem."

Roy walked up to Havoc, sticking his face next to the lit cigarette.

"Yipes, Colonel, careful! You'll burn yourself." Havoc yanked back his hand so as not to singe his superior officer's nose. "What gives?"

"Nothing," Roy said after a moment. He was thinking about the tobacco he had smelled earlier, by the hatch leading into the waterway. It didn't smell like Havoc's cigarette.

"Everything okay, sir?"

Roy stood with his hand on his chin, thinking. He had a hunch, but in the end, he decided he didn't want to say anything based on just a hunch. Actions came first. There would be time for thinking later.

Roy turned back to his men. "Change of plans. The chimeras aren't feral, and they didn't escape. They're attacking people to serve some purpose. First, we'll investigate the people whose blood was drained and figure out who to set our sights on next. I want Warrant Officer Falman and Master Sergeant Fuery to find someone with experience in analyzing blood. Get them cracking on samples from the victims. As soon as we narrow down our list of suspects, we'll move in. Tonight, if we can. The sooner the better!"

"Yes, sir!"

Roy saw his subordinates salute out of the corner of his eye as he stood mulling over the details of the case. It was a difficult problem to solve with the scraps of information available, but Roy had a keen analytical mind, and right now, every cylinder was firing, churning toward a solution.

"BLUEBERRIES!"

"Um . . . oranges!"

"Hey, that's the second time you said orange!"

"No way!"

"You said it yourself just now, Kip!"

Alphonse's and Kip's voices echoed off the cobblestones on the sunny sloping road. They were walking to deliver more picture books to the children living along the river and naming all the fruit they could think of to pass the time.

While searching the books in the cellar for *The Evolution of the Body,* Alphonse had come across a buried pile of picture books. Kip had mentioned that he would be going down to the river again that day, and Alphonse decided he would tag along and help. Alphonse and Edward had stayed up late the night before searching the stacks, so only a few remained. Edward offered to keep browsing the shelves while Alphonse went along with the boy.

Alphonse put the picture books he'd found in the cellar into a paper bag and slung it over his shoulder. In his other hand, he held half of the cardboard box by one of its rope handles. Kip held the other half to make sure it didn't spill.

"This is a whole lot of books. You always carry this many down here by yourself?" Alphonse asked, taking care not to let Kip carry the brunt of the weight. He had thought yesterday that the books filling the cardboard box looked thin, but with so many, it sure seemed like a heavy load for anyone, especially a little boy.

"Yeah. Some of the kids like stories about animals, and some of them like adventures. Some of them want to read the same book again, so they asked me to bring it back for them. That's why I always take so many."

"Huh, good for you," Alphonse said.

"But everyone's so happy, I don't mind at all," Kip continued, smiling.

"Well," Alphonse said, "I'm impressed. You're one of the nicest people I've met, Kip."

"I don't think so. Mom is much nicer than I am." Kip laughed, straining to hold his side of the box. "She always reads me lots of books! And when it's raining and I go to the river, she comes down to the bridge to meet me halfway. She even makes me hot milk."

"That's because Shelley's nice too," Alphonse said, remembering how the boy's foster mother had welcomed the two of them the day before, even offering them a place to stay.

"Well, Da—Luon, too, when he comes home. He's pretty nice. He plays with me a lot."

Kip had been on the verge of calling Luon "Dad." Alphonse had thought it only seemed odd to him and Edward that Kip called one of his foster parents "Mom," but not the other "Dad." However, it seemed that Kip was a bit confused about it too.

"I was wondering," Alphonse asked. "You never call Luon your dad, do you? Why not?"

"Well, he says that I shouldn't, because it's not nice to my real dad. But I always mess up. Shelley says I should just call him Dad anyway, but Luon always makes a face when I do."

Luon probably just had Kip's real parents' feelings in mind, but Alphonse could tell it made Kip sad. Even thinking about it brought a melancholy, far-off look to Kip's face. It was only for a moment, though. Soon, that familiar brightness returned to the boy's eyes.

"Hey, Alphonse, what are your parents like?"

Alphonse thought about the question for a moment before answering. "I remember my mom was really gentle. A little like Shelley, maybe."

"Yeah? Was she a good cook?"

"The best. She always made great food for us. And she made great cakes. What's Shelley's favorite dish?"

"Mom? Well . . ."

The two walked down the road, occasionally switching hands carrying the box, talking about their families as they went. They soon came to the river.

"I'll just be a minute," Kip said, putting his things down on the ground and taking the rest of the books from Alphonse.

"You sure you can carry all those? I'm happy to help!"

"No, it's fine. Maybe you can wait here?" Kip asked him, sounding a little embarrassed. Ishvalans had a healthy mistrust of strangers, Alphonse knew. He nodded and sat down on a flat rock next to the river.

Box and bag in hand, Kip walked toward the houses, the matchbox in his pocket rattling every time he jumped over a rock. Children came running out of the dilapidated houses. They were all Ishvalans, most about Kip's height. With shouts of glee, they tore into the stack of books he had brought. Kip handed the books over, exchanged a few words with some of the parents, and came right back.

"Thanks for waiting, Alphonse." Kip was dragging the cardboard box behind him as he walked. In it were picture books the children had already finished reading.

"Well, home then?"

"Yep," Kip nodded briskly, but a shadow had come over his face.

"Something wrong?" Alphonse asked. "I hope I didn't scare anyone?"

"No, not at all," Kip told him, still sounding a little glum.

Wondering what the matter was, but not wanting to pry, Alphonse picked up the box and walked toward the stone steps that would take them up from the river back to the streets. The steps were very high for a small child. Alphonse went up first, put down the box, then went back to carry Kip. When they were about to reach the top, Kip spoke from under Alphonse's arm.

"Do you think I shouldn't be living with Luon and Shelley?"

"Why?"

Alphonse was just lifting Kip up over the last section of wall. Worry filled the boy's red eyes as he stared down at him. Alphonse decided not to set him down beside the road but instead sat him on the wall.

"I don't think there's any problem with it. Did someone say you shouldn't?"

"Not really," Kip replied, looking down at his feet. "It's just, one of the fathers living down in the houses by the river said I should live with his family until my real parents are found."

"Why is that?"

"They say I won't stick out so much among the other Ishvalans. If I'm with them, life would be easier than up here with the Amestrians. But I don't know what to do . . ."

Alphonse thought he understood what the father was saying.

For that little excursion down to the river today, Kip had

put on his long-sleeved shirt and a big hood. Even though he wore a T-shirt inside the house, whenever he went outside, he put on longer clothes to hide his brown skin, even when the weather was hot like today.

That's what they meant by life being difficult up here.

"I didn't used to think it was a problem at all, me having different-colored eyes and everything. Everybody's a little different anyway, so what's the big deal? By then I made some Ishvalan friends, and we talked about books together, and I started coming down here to the river like this."

Alphonse listened silently.

"Then the grown-ups, they started telling me things. They said it's not just the color of our eyes. Amestrians and Ishvalans are different in other ways too, they say. They say I shouldn't be with them. I didn't understand what they meant at first, but now I'm starting to think maybe they're right."

"Why is that?"

"Well, when I walk through town by myself, everyone always gives me this sad look. It's almost like it's hard for them to be near me. Hey, do you think Luon and Shelley feel that too?"

Even as Kip was talking, a passing traveler noticed him and hurried away, a startled look on his face. Residents of the town were probably used to seeing Ishvalans, but Lambsear got its fair share of travelers. Alphonse and Edward, for that matter, had been a little confused when they first met Kip, not knowing how they should talk to him—or even if they should talk to him at all.

So people avoided the little boy from Ishval, not knowing that while they tried to give him his space, they were actually hurting him.

Kip sat on the wall, his fingers clenched, hands resting on his knees.

"Do I have to live away from Luon and Shelley because I'm Ishvalan?" he asked again. His little voice was trembling.

Kip looked on the verge of tears, and Alphonse wasn't sure what to say. He thought for a while, then knelt down before the boy. "Here, I want you to see something, Kip."

Taking care that no passersby were watching, Alphonse took his fingers and spread the plates of his armor suit.

"Huh?" Kip leaned closer, peering inside then jerked back in surprise. "Yipes!" Where he had expected to see Alphonse, he saw absolutely nothing. "Alphonse?"

Alphonse held a single upright finger to Kip's open mouth. "Shh. It's a secret, okay?"

"Where . . . where are you?"

"I'm right here," Alphonse told him, "but I'm invisible." It wasn't entirely the truth, but little Kip seemed to believe him. "Wow, an invisible man!"

Alphonse stood again. "Okay, here's a question for you."

Kip raised an eyebrow.

"My brother, Edward, is normal—people can see him—but I'm invisible. That makes us completely different. But we stick together, don't we? Why do you think that is?"

"Well, um . . ." Kip was caught a little off guard by the question, but he started thinking on it straightaway. "Because you're brothers?"

"Guess again!"

"Drat," Kip pouted.

Alphonse crouched until he was at Kip's eye level and raised a single finger. "The answer is, because I like him."

"You like him?"

"Yeah. I like my brother. And he likes me. That's why, even though we're different, we stay together."

It was the truth. That they were brothers helped, too, of course. But that alone didn't mean they had to choose to spend practically every day together, sharing good times and bad. Though they might fight and even come to blows sometimes, Alphonse never really disliked Edward. He was just too optimistic, too cool when he fought, and sometimes hilariously uncool. Alphonse didn't just like him as a brother, he liked him as a person.

He turned back to Kip. "Do you like Shelley?"

"I do."

"How about Luon?"

Kip smiled brightly. "A lot!" he shouted, grabbing Alphonse around the neck. "I like him a lot! I like both of them a lot! That's why I want to stay with them, Alphonse!"

"And stay with them you should. Being different from somebody isn't a good enough reason to leave. It's not a reason at all. I'm sure Luon and Shelley feel the same way about you."

Alphonse gave Kip a pat on the head, then pulled away. "That's right. I wanted to buy some souvenirs of Lambsear while we're here. You want to come with me?"

"Sure, sounds like fun!" Kip nodded, grinning.

"Let's go then!" Alphonse went to help Kip down from the wall when he stopped suddenly.

"Um, what I just said about my brother . . ."

Kip held a finger to Alphonse's mouth. "Shh. It's a secret. Right? Don't worry, I won't tell a soul!"

"Thanks!"

The two boys put their foreheads together, making a hollow bonking sound, then walked off down the street, laughing as they went.

MEANWHILE, Edward watched over the bookstore as a favor to Shelley while she was out shopping. It was the least he could do after he and his brother had spent the night for free.

The glass doors opened with a ringing of bells, and a young man with the look of a local student entered.

"Hello, there."

"Hiya." Edward greeted the customer without making eye contact while scanning a stack of books on the counter he had brought up from the cellar to check.

"No, that's not it, that's not it," he mumbled to himself. "Hey, another picture book . . . Nope that's not it, nor that one . . . Hey, is that a new guide to mineable ores?!"

Flipping the books to one side, and occasionally opening the ones that interested him, Edward busied himself with his stack, paying the customer no attention at all. Meanwhile, the student meekly walked around, checking the books on the first floor, then going up the walkway to check the books on the top shelves. Still Edward paid him no mind.

Finally, the young man approached the desk, shooting Edward meaningful glances, like he was looking for a book and wanted some help, but was too shy to say it. Finally, he spoke.

"Um . . ."

"Yeah? Can I help you?"

Edward tore his gaze away from a book and glanced at the student. At least, he meant for it to be a glance, but the glazed look in his eyes after staring at books for hours and the way the light caught his face made it look like a stone-cold glare.

The student swallowed. "No! Er, um . . . Yes! I'm looking for a dictionary, actually."

"Second floor, second shelf from the right, fifth shelf from the top. There's two of them."

After having spent a day and a half searching in these books, Edward knew the store like the back of his hand. A good bookseller would have gone to get the books for the customer himself, but the thought never occurred to Edward.

The student went back up the stairs to the walkway, found the books he was looking for, and paid.

"Thank you very much," the student said politely. He left with both dictionaries under his arm.

The next customers to enter the store were a neighborhood housewife and a young man.

"Where might I find books on cooking?"

"I'm looking for something on art history . . ."

Edward had just brought up a fresh batch from the cellar. "Not this one either . . . Grr . . . Where is that book?!" He glanced up. "Cookbooks are in the cellar. There are two on the seventh row from the top, second shelf from the left, and three more on the first floor. Art history is on the top shelf, second floor, five volumes . . . Hey, look, this one's signed! . . . If you can't reach something, the ladder's over there."

For a moment the two stood, utterly confused by Edward's scatterbrained monologue.

Of course, Edward was in the wrong. He should have been more attentive to his customers. Not that he was being rude on purpose. Just like when he sparred with Izumi, he became so intent on the task at hand, he simply forgot to be polite.

Soon he heard chuckling coming from the front of the shop. Edward had just finished checking his latest stack. He looked up to see Alphonse and Kip laughing in front of the glass doors.

"Ed!"

"Those customers sure looked surprised!"

The two had been watching Edward at work from the street.

"If you're going to watch the shop, you might try smiling a little," Alphonse said with a chuckle, walking into the store, his hands full of picture books.

Now that he thought about it, Edward admitted he might have been a little brusque. He *was* watching the store as a favor, after all. It wouldn't do to drive business away.

"Er, sorry about that," he said to Kip, but the boy didn't seem to mind.

"Don't worry about it. I'm just impressed that you remembered where all the books were! That was cool!"

"I don't remember exactly where they were, just sort of generally. Oh, Shelley's out shopping, but she said she left a snack for you in the kitchen."

"Really? I'll be right back!" Kip dashed through the back door out of the shop.

"Thanks for checking through the books, Ed," Alphonse said.

"Nah, thank you for going out with Kip."

"Well? Do you think Dr. Dell's book is in here anywhere?"

"Who knows." Edward frowned. He picked up a rare book he had found moments before. "There are some valuable, rare books in here, that's for sure. It might have already sold, or it might still be buried somewhere . . . Now that I've made it this far, I plan to check them all, of course."

"Yeah, we'd better. Just a little more to go. I'll go put these picture books down in Luon's study and come help you."

"I'll go with you. I found some picture books in the last stack to take up there."

Edward and Alphonse walked across the garden to the house and climbed the steps to Luon's study in the attic.

Luon's study had a large window at one end and bookshelves running along both sides. All of the picture books sat in the lower half of the shelves, so that Kip could reach them. The higher shelves remained open, probably for new acquisitions, except for the very top shelf, on which Luon had put his personal effects: memo pads, pens, boxes of erasers and such, and letters bound in small bundles. Everything had dust on it, revealing just how infrequently he came home.

Shelley had shown them the study the night before, when they determined there were no books there other than the picture books. A desk in the corner had drawers in it, but all of them were too small to hold a large book like the one they were looking for.

Edward sat on the floor, sticking picture books onto the shelf wherever he could find a space. Alphonse sat in front of the bookshelf across the room, doing the same for all of the books the kids living along the river had returned.

"The bottom three shelves are getting kind of crowded," Edward grumbled, searching for an open spot.

"You could put them on the shelf above that."

"Well, I'm not certain Kip . . . can . . . reach . . . that . . . high," Edward said, struggling to push another book into an already full shelf. "Grr . . . get in there!"

Suddenly, the book gave up resisting and slid in. It hit the back with such force the whole shelf rocked precariously.

"Yikes!"

Edward held up his hands to shield himself from the rain of memo pads and stationery from the top of the shelf.

"Oops . . ."

Edward quickly began gathering up the fallen pens and pieces of paper.

Alphonse came over to help, carefully straightening a bent notepad and righting a spilled box of pencils.

"I appreciate you wanting to keep the books within Kip's reach, but if you jam them in there so tight like that, he won't be able to pull them out," Alphonse noted.

"Good point. Ack, look at all these letters that fell down. I hope these weren't in any kind of order." Edward began restacking the letters, checking the front and back for post-marked dates.

"This one's from five years ago, and here's one from last year, and—Hey!" Edward was scanning the postmarks when he came across a line of words that made his eyes open wide and his mouth gape in astonishment. "Whoa!" he yelled. "Al, look at this letter!"

"Ed, we really shouldn't be reading someone else's . . ." Alphonse began.

Edward shoved a letter in front of his eyes. "No, look at the sender!"

"Huh? Hey!"

On the letter, the name *Balerea Dell* was written in precise pen strokes.

Edward and Alphonse stared at each other.

It was against every rule they knew to read someone else's mail.

Edward didn't let it stop him long. For him, getting Alphonse back his original body superseded all other concerns.

" . . . I know you're not supposed to do this, but we have to read this letter!" Edward slid the letter out of its envelope.

Mr. Luon Egger,

I read your letter with great interest.

I think we would make excellent partners, do you not agree?

Your help would be of great assistance to me.

Please find the address of my laboratory below. I would like to speak with you at greater length.

Balerea Dell

"So Luon and Dr. Dell worked together!" Edward snapped his fingers. "I'll bet Luon read Dr. Dell's book when he found it in his house and then sent him a letter! He might have been looking for more books!"

It would make sense for Dell to want contact with Luon, a bookseller, as well. With one banned book to his name already, he would need all of the connections he could get if he wanted to publish anything else in the future.

However, this seemed to be the only letter from Dr. Dell. Perhaps they hadn't been able to come to an arrangement, and this was the end of their communication. However, it was still an incredible stroke of luck for Edward and Alphonse. They might not have found *The Evolution of the Body*, but if they could talk to the author himself, who needed the book?

The letter was dated three years ago. Dr. Dell might well still be at the address. Edward committed it to memory and returned the letters to the shelf.

"Let's go meet the good doctor!"

Even if Dr. Dell wasn't willing to share his research with complete strangers, they could at least begin a conversation that might help them in their search.

"Even the slightest clue toward getting back your body is good enough!"

"Right!"

This was the chance Edward and Alphonse had been looking for. They spent the next ten minutes grinning and high-fiving each other. ✸

CHAPTER 3

MEETINGS AND ENCOUNTERS

STARS SPARKLED IN THE SKY, decorating the night. Soft moonlight lit the trees, their leaves rustling in the wind. There, in the deep mountain night, stood Balerea Dell's mansion.

The red brick walls and high, pointed roof were weathered with age. A bronze bell hung by the front door with a slender chain that guests could ring to announce their presence.

"Good evening! Hello?" Edward shouted, yanking on the chain. Next to him, Alphonse stood looking at the windows on the upper floor.

"None of the lights are on, Ed."

"Still kind of early for him to be sleeping . . . Dell better not have moved!"

Edward gave the bell chain another tug.

Dell's house was a considerable distance from Lambsear, but not so far that they couldn't jump on a train and be there by nightfall. If they couldn't find Dell, they planned on returning to their book search in short order, so they excused themselves with a suitable story to Shelley and Kip and promised they'd be back soon.

Edward rang the bell another five or six times. There was no answer. The old house looked abandoned, but the handle on the door seemed well used.

"Well, it looks like someone's still living here," Edward said. On a whim, he reached out and gave the doorknob a yank. It clicked.

"Huh?"

"It's not locked."

Edward and Alphonse gingerly pushed on the door and stuck in their heads. Moonlight spilled in through large windows, filling the interior with a pale, bluish light. The main hall had a hardwood floor, the lines between the planks forming an elegant pattern. Small tables sat here and there adorned with unlit lamps. There was a staircase going up directly ahead of them and a fireplace on either side of the room. Several doors led out to other rooms, and corridors led to the left and to the right. One doorway on the left looked as though it led down another staircase to some kind of cellar. It was a very large mansion.

"Good evening!" Edward shouted. *"Good evening!"* an echo replied.

He walked in, picking up one of the lamps near the door. The wick of the alcohol lamp was still warm. "Someone was here recently. There are still hot embers in the fireplace. Looks

like they were burning something more than just wood here."
Edward picked up a poker and made to thrust it into the coals
when a loud sound came from below his feet.

FWUMP!

The floorboards shuddered. It sounded like something
heavy had fallen directly beneath them.

"What was that?"

"Dr. Dell must be pretty old by now, right? What if something's fallen on him?" Alphonse said worriedly. "Let's go
check it out, Ed!"

"Right!"

The brothers charged for the stairs, snatching a box of
matches and a lamp from one of the tables to light their way
down the stone steps.

An iron door at the bottom of the stairs blocked their
passage. The door was shut firmly and locked with a padlock.

"It's been locked from the outside . . . which means no one's
in there, right?" Edward fingered the padlock, when beside
him, Alphonse gasped in surprise.

"Ed!"

"What?"

"E-Ed, look!" Alphonse was pointing down at the floor.

Edward followed his finger down then reflexively jumped
back a whole three feet. "What the heck?!"

A deep red liquid spilled out from beneath the door,
pooling at the bottom of the stairs. It looked viscous, sticky.
It looked like . . .

"Blood!"

"What if someone's hurt?!"

"Al, hold this!"

Edward thrust his lamp toward Alphonse, and clapping his hands together, he touched the door. A bright flash of lightning illuminated the stairwell. The glow ran around the outlines of the door for an instant. When it cooled, another smaller door had formed within the first.

Edward grabbed the newly formed handle of his alchemical door. It opened smoothly, and the two brothers leapt inside, expecting the worst.

There was no one in the room, but what they did find was beyond belief. The papers and glass strewn about the large underground chamber were lit by the lamp in Alphonse's hand. An alchemical circle had been drawn on the floor, upon which rested several large cylindrical tanks. Powder spilled from alchemical urns and vials scattered on a row of tables, and a large bookshelf had fallen on its side. Though the light from the lamp didn't illuminate the entire room, from what they saw, they could guess the chaos extended all the way to the far wall, lost in shadow.

More than the destruction, what shocked Edward was the vast quantity of dark red liquid filling the transparent tanks and beakers.

"What is this place?"

"Is all that . . . blood?!"

One of the tanks had fallen over, spilling across the floor near the entrance.

Edward picked up a beaker and turned it on its side. The thick, red liquid spilled out on the desk, spreading in a slow circle. Some chemical or alchemical process had been used to keep the blood from coagulating, apparently. Its viscous appearance and cloying scent were enough to convince him this was the real thing.

"Just what is Dell up to?"

Edward walked around the laboratory, picking up scattered papers as he went. "'What comprises the human body but blood and flesh? Without flowing blood, the body would rot, a truth we can see in the recently developed blood transfusion technology. The blood fights bacterial invaders to the body, closes external wounds, keeps the body alive . . .'"

Drops of blood stained the handwritten pages of the research notes Edward found on the floor. At the bottom of one, he could make out a signature: *Balerea Dell.*

"Hey, Ed, I found a report here," Alphonse said, picking some papers up from another spot in the room. "'By applying alchemy to the blood, one can invigorate the cells, preventing decomposition of the flesh and spurring growth.'"

The two picked up paper after paper, reading them by the light of their flickering lamp.

Only a portion of the most detailed report remained, but for Edward and Alphonse, who had spent days of their life since early childhood poring over mountains of alchemical lore, it was easy to see what he had been researching.

"So he used alchemy to augment blood and heighten the body's capacity for regeneration and growth." Edward looked up from the papers. "Blood carries nutrients to the cells. It's just like transfusion. He must have concluded that if you strengthen the blood and heighten the body's regenerative ability, you could grow limbs like a lizard grows back its tail."

"Just the kind of thing a man who's both an alchemist and a doctor would think up."

"No kidding. If he used it in his treatments at all, it might have been a wild success . . ."

Edward and Alphonse gazed over the wreckage of the laboratory.

The two of them were more than enthusiastic about advancing the science of medicine. However, one look at this laboratory told them something here was terribly wrong. As evidence, they had a vast quantity of blood and a row of large vats along the wall, their contents preserved in formaldehyde.

In the first vat, they saw a lizard, or something very similar, but its shape was all wrong. It had scales but also wings. In the vat next to it, a snake with six claws extruding from its belly curled in what might once have been pain. They were all chimeras.

"It looks like he was able to strengthen blood with his alchemy, and that worked fine, but then the blood started acting on its own, grabbing other creatures, trying to expand, to grow. It got greedy."

The vats were labeled, and a notebook sitting nearby detailed the daily progress of the experiment. Apparently, the chimeras had been an unexpected byproduct, but not an unwanted one. Few things were as valuable as chimeras when studying the body. A large incubator sat in one corner of the room, and in one larger cistern, a giant chimera, still half formed, floated in a pool of blood.

"So he found out how to make chimeras without actually planning them. I wonder if he gave up his original research when he realized he couldn't use alchemy on blood already in the body . . ."

"No, he didn't," Edward said, shaking the beaker he had emptied onto the desk. "He moved on to something else. Take a look."

Alphonse looked down at the puddle of blood on the table. Something floated in it. It looked like a rat's tail.

"He wasn't augmenting the blood inside a rat to grow back a tail. He was putting a tail inside augmented blood and trying to grow a rat."

The rat's tail looked as though it had a bit of new growth at one end. Perhaps he thought if he continued in this line, he would eventually be able to create anything out of a single cell. Turn the process around with perfectly augmented blood, and he could administer his technique to a grown person to fix injuries and illness.

Edward read the writing along the edge of one of the report pages. "*. . . I must perfect my augmented blood, no matter what the cost.*"

From their brief survey, it seemed that when Dr. Dell had written *The Evolution of the Body*, his research had been a little on the comfortable side of sanity. Still, it was a risky enough field that someone saw the potential for danger in it, and so he had been kicked out of the academy. Clearly, however, that had not stopped him. According to his journal, he had been trying to apply his new techniques to humans, as well as working on strengthening human blood for several months now.

With a banned book hanging over him, Dr. Dell had no recourse but to further his research in secrecy. Which begged the question: where was he getting all this blood?

"No matter what the cost . . ."

The evidence of that cost lay in pools, jars, and vats all around them. No hospital or research laboratory would willingly share its stock with someone like Dell. Which meant that all this blood had been obtained illegally. Dell no longer cared about the advancement of medicine. His lust for research had led him down a different path.

"I hoped we might find some clues that would help us, but this . . ."

"Yeah . . ."

Edward and Alphonse saw that Izumi had been right all along, and it took the wind out of their sails. They were no strangers to this: chasing after a clue, only to track it down and find that it offered them nothing. Still, they had to be sure, to see it with their own eyes. They had to defy their teacher, they had to search for that book, all so that they could put this clue to rest and get on with finding the next.

Rather than disappointment, they felt relief to finally know the truth. There was nothing for them here.

"Maybe Luon stopped writing after that first letter because he found out how dangerous Dell's research was."

"Yeah. Who would want books about this kind of research in his bookstore, anyway?"

Edward picked up the lamp and began walking between the tables toward the cellar door. "I guess we should tell the army about all this. They love cracking down on mad scientists."

Although he was officially a part of the army, Edward generally kept to himself about things that didn't concern him directly. Still, he couldn't allow dangerous experiments like these to continue.

"I wonder where Dr. Dell got to? It seems like he—or some-one—was here not too long ago. From the way everything's scattered around, it's almost like someone bolted out of here fast, probably because they were afraid of being discovered."

"Yeah. I'm still wondering where all this blood came from."

"You're not the only one. I suppose he could have bought it from a hospital . . . You know, for transfusions?"

"I don't know. I read that hospitals are running low help-ing all the people who've been attacked by those chimeras. It doesn't seem likely they'd sell some research scientist all this—"

Alphonse stopped, his own words triggering something in the back of his mind. Edward had come to the same conclusion on his own. The brothers looked at each other.

FWOMP!

Another loud noise sounded in the air, this one coming from right behind them. What vials still stood on the desks rattled in their racks.

Edward whirled and lifted his lantern high.

They had been so distracted by the blood and report pages lying around the laboratory that they had missed a door at the very back of the room.

FWOMP! FWOMP!

Something was slamming against the door. This time, it wasn't a single thump but repeated strikes, followed by an unearthly howl. Then the howl was joined by the sound of something—many somethings—barking.

"Al," Edward said, gingerly stepping back away toward the exit. "Can I ask you a question?"

"Is it the same thing I'm asking myself right now?"

"You think those chimeras in formaldehyde, Dell's research with all this blood, and these chimera attacks are all related somehow?"

"You bet I do. Can I ask you a question?"

"Shoot."

"That noise we're hearing, those things on the other side of the door. Those are more chimeras, aren't they?"

As if in response, the door splintered into pieces, and a pack of twisted, horrid creatures hurtled into the room.

"Yikes! Look at all of them!"

"Run, Ed!"

It would be too dangerous to face so many chimeras down there, with just one lantern as their only source of light. Edward and Alphonse beat a hasty retreat out through the door to the stairs.

The chimeras chasing them were unlike the wolves they had encountered in Dublith. These were all formed from different combinations: there was one like a bear with an exceedingly long tail, one had a third eye on its forehead, and another looked like a rabbit with impossibly sharp talons and a long, crooked beak.

Edward and Alphonse dashed up the stairs, the chimeras hot on their heels. One caught up to them and opened its jaw to take a chunk out of Edward's shoulder. Its fangs were long and sharp, as befitted a creature designed to suck blood, and saliva snaked in a long line from its red tongue.

Edward quickly fashioned a blade out of his right arm, cut the thing aside, and ran out into the hall just as more chimeras came bounding out of one of the side rooms. Two more already stood in the entrance, baring their fangs as they stared hungrily at Edward and Alphonse.

"This doesn't look good . . ."

Dell had been using the other rooms for his research too, apparently, not just the cellar. Through the open doors, Edward could see more tables, vials, and vats.

"Ed, you can't fight them at close range! They're after blood!" Alphonse shouted, hurling a chimera to the side. Alphonse, being a suit of armor, was at little risk of injury from these creatures, but if one sank its teeth into Edward, he was finished.

"Dammit!" Edward retracted his right arm-blade and reached for a nearby chair. A sharp light flashed in the moonlit hall, and a long spear formed from Edward's hand where the chair had been. "We'll go look for an exit on the other side!"

"Okay!"

Edward and Alphonse ran for the corridor at the back left of the room, heading deeper into the mansion. As one, the chimera pack gave chase. Edward paused to knock a winged beast out of the air with his spear. Next to him, Alphonse took down one like a snarling warthog with a well-placed roundhouse kick.

Within moments, the hall was filled with the yelping and screaming of injured chimeras. Still, they attacked with such ferocity that Edward and Alphonse didn't even have time to check the rooms on either side of the corridor. Not that it would have helped if they opened a door only to find another laboratory filled with chimeras waiting behind it.

The chimeras they had met in Dublith were wary, but these were merely violent, and they attacked with single-minded

fury. No windows lined the corridor walls, and the farther down the hall they went, the dimmer the light became.

"There's no end to these things!"

A chimera clamped down on Edward's spear. He kicked it and the spear away, then clapped his hands together and dropped to his knees. When his palms touched the floor, another dazzling light shone in the dim hall, and a wall rose beneath Edward's hands. Even as it did, the chimeras kept coming.

One of the horrible creatures was caught in the wall itself. It lashed with its claws at Edward and Alphonse, blood streaming from cuts the wall carved in its belly. Yet even as they watched, the creature's wounds faded, torn flesh becoming whole.

"That must be an effect of the augmented blood!"

"Let's put some distance between us and them while we have a chance!"

Edward and Alphonse ran down the corridor as fast as they could. It seemed impossibly long, in part because the dim light made it difficult to judge distances. They had only run a few moments when they could make out a wall blocking off the corridor ahead of them.

From behind them came the sound of Edward's wall crumbling. They looked back to see the eyes of the chimeras gleaming with an evil light as they rushed toward them.

"A dead end!"

"Time for another door!" Edward extended his hand as he ran, while Alphonse stood his ground behind him. He would have to buy Edward a few seconds' time to make the door.

"Which will it be? A door to freedom or a door into another chimera lab . . ."

Whichever it was, anything was better than being stuck where they were. Edward raised his hands and touched the wall. But an instant before he could work his alchemy, a bolt of lightning shot across the wall.

"Whaa—?!"

Edward shielded his eyes from the blinding light. When it faded, he saw a door forming in the wall. Before Edward could fully comprehend what had happened, the door opened and a hand reached out, pulling him through.

"Whoa!"

Edward was on the other side before he could even see who pulled him through. He found himself tossed onto the floor. Edward looked up to see a tall, shadowed figure standing over him. Behind the silhouette, Alphonse was facing off with the chimeras. At the last possible moment, this shadowy figure yanked Alphonse back too and closed the door behind him. When the door shut, they were in utter darkness. Edward guessed they were in some sort of storage room or pantry.

Whoever the mysterious man was, he was an alchemist, and he had just saved Edward and Alphonse. A frightening series of thumps echoed through the room as the chimeras collided with the other side of the door, but the door held.

"What do you think you're doing? This is no place for children!" the man's voice said, low and sharp.

Edward squinted his eyes, trying to see in the darkness. "Who's there?!" he called out, but he recognized the voice. It was the same as the one that had spoken when he encountered the chimeras back in Dublith, the one that had shouted "Stop!" Back in Dublith, Edward had thought the voice belonged to some concerned citizen on the street, shouting a warning to him, but now there was no mistaking it. Whomever this was, he was moving with the chimeras. The voice sounded too young to belong to Dr. Dell, though. Maybe this was his assistant.

"Who are you? Are you working with Dr. Dell?" The mysterious man gave no answer, which Edward took to be affirmation. "Why did you save us? Why not let the chimeras finish us off?" asked Alphonse, still wondering who this man was. He hadn't been there when Edward ran into him in Dublith.

"I have no intention of involving innocents in this," the man answered.

"Innocents? What about all the people whose blood got drained? Were they involved?"

"Maybe not, but it's no concern of yours. You kids should leave, now."

That did it. The color slowly rose in Edward's face, and then he snapped.

"Who are you calling kids?! And where do you get off acting all high and mighty after what you've done? You'll be singing a different song once the army gets its hands on you!"

"Sorry, but that's not going to happen." The man's voice was cold and hard. "There's a door out of here in the back. Forget this place and go home," he said evenly. It was clear the damage wrought by his chimeras didn't weigh heavily on his conscience.

Edward glared through the darkness in the man's direction. "So you're an alchemist? Is that why you think you can give us the brush-off? Well, I'm sorry to inform you, but both my brother and I know a thing or two about alchemy. We're taking you in, even if we have to use force."

"Kids doing alchemy? What's the world coming to?" the man said, sounding a bit surprised but still unwavering. "It's too dangerous to stay here. Leave before you get hurt."

"Dangerous—" Edward began, when a loud roar drowned him out.

The chimeras in the hall howled in unison. The sounds of scratching at the door ceased. Edward and Alphonse could hear the chimeras running back into the large hall, away from their hiding place.

"What's going on out there?"

Edward and Alphonse scratched their heads in the silence left by the chimeras' departure. Suddenly, a tremendous booming noise sounded directly above their heads.

"Whoa!"

The mansion shook, and something struck Edward's shoulder with a glancing blow. It was a piece of the ceiling.

Alphonse and Edward quickly covered their heads with their arms. They could hear gunshots and the howling of the chimeras.

"Gunfire? Could that be the army?!"

"I hoped they wouldn't start so soon . . ." the man said. "Stay here and you'll be caught between the chimeras and the guns!"

The man grabbed Edward and Alphonse by the arms and pushed them toward the exit at back of the room.

"Ouch!" Edward yelped, running into a wall. The impact knocked the silver watch dangling out of his pocket. Edward rubbed his throbbing forehead.

Outside, the barrage continued. The door, once Edward found it, vibrated with every shell fired into the mansion. Apparently, the building was older than it looked. Already, the structure ached and groaned under the stress, and the doorway was swaying dangerously.

The howling of the chimeras and the gunshots echoed in the dark room. From the sounds of it, the army was using rifles and grenades now. The cacophony of gunshots and explosions mingled with the screaming of the chimeras.

Now the mansion itself began to slant and tilt to one side. One of the walls collapsed, and the door began to splinter. Moonlight suddenly came streaming into the pitch-black room, glinting on Edward's silver pocket watch.

"That watch!" came a surprised voice from behind him. "You . . . you're a state alchemist?"

Edward looked around to see the man who had saved them standing in the light for the first time. He was standing in front of the door he had created moments earlier, staring at Edward's watch.

"Luo—"

He saw the face only for a moment before the man stepped back into the shadows.

"How does a kid like you become a state alchemist?!" the man asked. Edward was so stunned and offended that, before he could even form a retort, the man disappeared into the darkness of the mansion.

"H-Hey!"

Edward shouted after the man, but chasing him was no longer an option. The army had brought out its cannons now. Before Edward's eyes, the outside wall of the mansion was being systematically blown to smithereens.

"Yipes!"

"Ed, we need to take cover!"

"What are they trying to do, take down the whole mansion with those chimeras? Whoever's running this operation is insane!"

Edward dodged a falling chunk of debris and ran for safety with his brother.

THE INSANE INDIVIDUAL in charge of running the operation stood across the garden from Dell's residence, watching the great mansion slowly implode on itself with great satisfaction.

"I'd call the first stage a success."

They had tried a more measured approach in dealing with the chimeras, but when the chimeras started pouring out, one after the other, Roy decided the quickest and simplest solution was to take down the entire place and the chimeras with it.

Thanks to the diligent research of his subordinates, they had narrowed down the suspect to one man—a former authority on blood research and an alchemist: Balerea Dell. Once they knew who they were after, the operation began in earnest.

Roy's team had already determined that Dell's most likely route of escape would lead him to the sturdy cellar beneath the mansion. They would bring the house down on top of him and worry about gathering evidence and apprehending their suspect after. When the howling of beasts and the sounds of gunfire ceased ringing through the night, Roy gave his orders.

"Havoc, I want you to check for any suspicious activity around the perimeter! Breda's team will load up and get in there! I want the rest of you on the lookout for more chimeras! Anyone with a free hand, help Hawkeye gather up the remaining laboratory materials!"

As his men raced off toward their duties, weaving through the bodies of the chimeras lying everywhere, Roy attended to the dossier in his hand.

"Balerea Dell . . ."

The dossier contained all the information the military had about Dr. Dell. He had investigated the use and alteration of blood in promoting human regeneration and achieved brief fame as a published author. But his biggest book had been stamped out under pressure from the academy and the military.

"Seeing as how there's not even a copy listed in the National Library, whatever he wrote must really have struck a nerve," Roy muttered to himself as he flipped through the dossier. He began paying particular attention to entries describing Dell's alchemical pursuits.

"Hmm . . . he specialized in medical alchemy, not in materials."

Roy fished in his pocket and pulled out a small pebble. It had been part of the wall that had blocked off the underground waterway.

Alchemy always leaves faint traces of its work, a residue. The less skilled the alchemist, the bigger the footprint, and hastily done alchemy is even more obvious. Yet Roy found hardly any traces at all on the pebble from the wall they had discovered—a wall that must have been erected on the fly to keep pursuers away from the chimeras.

Several buildings had collapsed during the chimera attacks, and examination of the wreckage revealed traces of alchemy there, too. Someone had used alchemy to weaken those buildings and topple them at near instant speed, stopping the creatures from attacking people other than their intended targets. Whoever was behind this, they were clearly a material alchemist, and that ruled out Dell. It was another alchemist— and a good one at that.

Roy sat in silence with his chin in his hand, lost in thought, when he became aware of someone calling his name.

"Colonel!"

He looked up to see Havoc standing gun in hand with a wry smile on his face. "I've received claims of, ah, excessive force, sir. Think you can deal with them?"

"'Claims'?" Roy inquired, looking over to where Havoc was pointing with his thumb. A little way off stood the Elric brothers.

"That was you blowing everything sky high back there, Colonel? I should've known!" Edward said, his black mood coloring his voice.

"Now this *is* a surprise," Roy called back. "And here I thought the chimeras were the only dangerous animals in these parts."

Edward walked closer, baring his teeth. "Watch who you call an animal, sir. You might get bitten!"

"Long time no see, Colonel," Alphonse joined in, making a last-ditch attempt to be cordial.

"You're looking good as always," Roy replied with a grin.

"What's the big idea, firing cannons into that house?! You almost buried us along with the rest of the place!" Edward's face was covered with soot from their close call. Though they had gotten out before it collapsed, falling debris had made their run a harrowing experience. Edward had immediately begun complaining about the clearly insane man in charge of the operation when he spotted Havoc and followed him back to Roy. "Or have we revised our standard search procedure?"

"We did give due warning, for what it's worth," Roy said, waving his hand at a loudspeaker on the ground behind him. He had shouted a warning of the incoming attack before they began firing on the mansion. However, Edward and Alphonse had been too engrossed in their fight with the chimeras to hear. "You can hardly blame us. Why should we expect anyone not directly involved in this mess to be out here in the mountains?"

Edward pouted his lips. "Well, we had work to do out here!"

"I see that." Roy knew of Edward and Alphonse's search for a way to restore their original bodies, and he had a pretty good idea of what had brought them to Dell's laboratory. "So you heard about Dell's research somewhere and came to check it out for yourself, eh? And in the end, you found out there was nothing useful for you here at all. Am I right?"

"Pretty much. Except you left out the part about you trying to add insult to injury with those cannons of yours. Real pleasant, that was."

"Now, now," Roy said, patting Edward on the shoulder and leading him farther away from the mansion so as not to interfere with Havoc and the others' work. "Sorry to talk shop after not seeing you for so long, but can you tell me anything about the inside?"

"Go look for yourself."

"Ed . . ."

"Ah ha ha. I see Fullmetal is as stubborn as ever. Of course, if you refuse to cooperate, I'll have you detained as possible conspirators with Dell."

"Do you smile like that when you torture all your victims, or is it something you reserve just for me?"

Still grumbling, Edward began to describe what they had seen in the laboratory, from the strange vats to the man they had met in the darkness.

"So it sounds like the doctor caught wind of our arrival and flew the coop. And his partner was in there?" Roy crossed his arms. "Based on what you say, I'd guess he left all the chimeras he didn't need as an ambush for us. This augmented blood of his is obviously fabulous for spurring quick growth and regeneration. He probably took the chimeras specifically designed for collecting blood along with him. He may be making even more as we speak, which means the next attack will come soon."

"You mean the chimeras will be attacking more people?" Alphonse asked worriedly.

Roy shook his head. "He's not sending them to attack just anyone. In fact, we know who his next target is. We'll be protecting the target and seeing if we can find out where Dell is setting up his next laboratory."

"What are you doing out here on the front lines, anyway, Colonel?" Edward asked suddenly. It didn't make sense for the commanding officer at Eastern to be all the way out here in the mountains, leading a mission like this.

Roy only smiled. "I have my reasons. Well now, once we're done casing this place, we'll go take up that guard duty I was talking about. Where are you two off to? I won't lie, we'd appreciate the help if you chose to stick with us."

"This has got nothing to do with me," Edward said, sticking out his tongue. "We'll head back to Lambsear, I figure. Someone's taken us in there, and they'll be expecting us."

Roy's eyes widened slightly, and he laughed. "Well isn't that a coincidence, Fullmetal. We'll be seeing each other again sooner than you think. As it turns out, I'm headed to Lambsear myself. The one we're supposed to guard is Brigadier General Bason."

"You're guarding Bason? That useless excuse for an officer? What, is he the next target on the list? Why?"

"Maybe it's because he's a useless excuse, like you say. And he's got a bad attitude to boot," Roy added casually. He turned to the truck parked behind them. "Look, I'll give you a ride into town. Consider it an apology for shooting at you. Just give me a minute here."

"Thanks, but no, thanks! Al, let's go!" Edward frowned and whirled away. He was already heading down the mountain, when Roy called out from behind.

"Wait up. There's one more thing I want to check with you."

"Yeah?" Edward grumbled in reply. Then he noticed that Roy's face was more serious than usual. "What? What is it?"

"Just now, you told me there was another alchemist besides Dr. Dell inside, right?"

"Yeah?"

"You sure you didn't see his face?"

Edward and Alphonse had told Roy about the man they had met in the mansion, but they had left out the part where they saw who he was. Finally, Edward cursed himself for looking aside when he had told Roy the story. The colonel's keen eyes rarely missed an obvious lie like that.

". . . We didn't see anything," Edward replied, wilting under Roy's stare. Alphonse remained silent. "Even if I did catch a glimpse, I don't remember what he looked like. I was too busy running for my life before someone brought the mansion down on my head."

"Right. Understood," Roy shrugged and waved. "Well, see you in Lambsear."

"Not if we see you first! Later!"

Edward and Alphonse turned and walked down the hill.

Hawkeye walked up beside Roy, who stood seeing the two brothers off.

"There's something we're not being told, isn't there?"

"That's my guess."

"No, I meant there's something you're not telling us, Colonel."

Roy glanced over to see Hawkeye, her expression calm as ever, staring back at him.

"You're sharp."

"He's someone you know?" She didn't ask who.

Roy nodded. ". . . Maybe."

Roy turned back to look at the collapsed heap of rubble where the mansion had stood. There, beneath the cool slanting light of the moon, smoke rose from the rubble, mingled with another familiar scent that hung in the air, reminding him of days long past.

A TOWN STOOD IN RUINS, a steady night breeze cooling its houses of cracked stone and abandoned factories. Its streets, lined with flower boxes, had been built to support the passage of many feet, but now the town was deserted, and the windows of its houses were broken. Sand filled the flower boxes, where now not even weeds grew.

A single light flared in this long-abandoned town.

It came from the window of a five-story factory building. Inside, an old man in a white laboratory coat walked to and fro, leaning on his cane for support. Brushing aside his long white whiskers when they got in the way, he stroked his beard with a wrinkled hand. Though his eyes as he peered at a flask filled with fluid were sunken, they still contained a lively spark.

"Yes, yes. I'll use this method to mix some fresh blood, do a little alchemy, and then we'll have it!" The old man cackled, talking to himself. It was Balerea Dell.

He picked a single bottle up from his desk and held it in his hand. "What's this? Used blood? That won't do; it must be fresh, fresh! Have we no more fresh blood?" Dell set the bottle down and resumed his pacing when the door opened behind him. The smoke that drifted into the room was greeting enough. Dell spoke without turning around.

"You're late. Well? Did my chimeras deal with the men at the laboratory? Fitting fate for those who would meddle with my research!" he said, loudly punctuating his words with a cackle. "While the army is busy with that dead end, I'll finish my augmented blood here, in my second laboratory!"

"They'll find this place too. It's only a matter of time," the man standing by the door said quietly. He was wearing a black shirt and dark green pants, and light brown hair fell haphazardly across his brow above gray eyes. His name was Luon Egger.

"What did you say?" asked Dell, finally turning around. "They'll find us?"

"Eastern Command sent their best. He'll find your laboratory, be sure of that."

"Friend of yours?"

Luon didn't answer, instead taking a drag on his cigarette and puffing out a cloud of smoke.

"No matter," Dell said. "I was just making more chimeras for defense. All I need to do now is finish my augmented blood before they come for me. Look at it! I have a test sample here, into which I've placed one of my fingernails. See? A complete finger, up to the knuckle! The structural formula you came up with was a great help, actually."

Dell cackled once more, pulling a small fleshy lump out of one of his test beakers and showing it to Luon. It was a severed fingertip, about an inch long and dripping red blood.

"My augmented blood will be finished soon. Then they'll remember me. They'll know my true potential! But I do need blood. Get some. Anyone's will do."

"Anyone?" Luon said, raising an eyebrow, but Dell didn't notice.

"I need it now. I'm sure you can pull one hundred cubic centimeters from a child with no problem. Or just take it all, it makes little difference to me. I'll need it for the next stage of tests, anyway. Oh, but what progress I could make if we could only harvest a hundred people at a time!"

Luon dropped his cigarette, rubbing it out on the floor beneath his heel, and walked up beside Dell. Taking a syringe from the table, he stuck it in his own arm. The thin glass tube filled with bright crimson blood.

"We decided you would choose your targets from the list. Never talk about taking from children again, ever," Luon said in a low voice. He drew the amount of blood Dell needed and tossed the syringe onto the desk.

"Hmph," Dell snorted. "It really doesn't matter who we take it from, you know. Scientifically speaking." A dribble of spit rolled down the old man's chin. He wiped it away and frowned, but soon his eyes gleamed when he saw the color of fresh blood in the syringe. Emptying its contents into a beaker, he resumed his experiment.

"So righteous you are, only wanting to take from the 'bad.' And I disagree with your policy of leaving our targets enough blood to live on. It's inefficient."

Dell placed the beaker in the middle of an alchemical circle, and at once the blood began to bubble, as though it were boiling. The old man kept an eye on the beaker while gathering papers that had fallen to the floor, using his cane to push them into a pile. Hundreds of names had been written on the papers, most of them crossed out. Dell jabbed his cane at the few remaining.

"This one's next. Go get blood from this Bason fellow in Lambsear. It's not far."

Luon stood silently.

"He's on the list. I can't see why you'd disapprove?" Dell questioned, glaring at the younger man. "You know I need fresh blood. If you don't like it, I'll release the chimeras and have them attack anyone they please. Understood? Oh, and when you're back, I'll need a little help with my research." Dell cackled again. "We are like brothers, you know, bound by our love for science, our shared dream! Together, we shall make our dream a reality!" Dell lifted his arms toward the ceiling, as though he were having a religious epiphany, while next to him, the blood in the beaker sloshed and bubbled.

KIP'S BRIGHT VOICE greeted the brothers upon their return from the Dell mansion. "Welcome back, you two!"

Kip had been reading picture books while he watched over the store, but now he looked up and closed his book. Edward and Alphonse could hear the sound of a knife chopping from the back—probably Shelley getting dinner ready.

"Finished your errand? You're back pretty late . . . Was it tough?"

"Well, a lot happened," Edward replied vaguely. In fact, they had arrived back in Lambsear around noon but had spent the next few hours sitting by the station, thinking, until the sky began to darken and they headed for the bookshop.

Smiling, Kip ran up to Edward and Alphonse where they stood at the entrance. "Hey, guess what? I went down to the river today, and remember that box you made for me, with the rope? It was great! I can carry the books all by myself!" Kip pointed to the box, sitting in the doorway, as he related the day's adventures to them. "Also, someone who used to live near my real parents is coming to meet me tomorrow. Maybe she knows where they are now? If she does, we have to tell Luon! He's been looking for them for so long."

Edward and Alphonse were unable even to nod in reply. Not after they had seen who was helping Dell at his mansion. They had told Roy they didn't get a clear view, but that had been a lie. That brief moment when the moonlight came streaming through a hole in the ceiling had been enough to see his face.

He looked just like the photo that hung on the wall of the Eggers' house, the one where he stood smiling next to a happy

Kip. Looking at Kip standing there now, without the faintest idea what his adopted father was really doing, Edward and Alphonse didn't know what to say. So they said nothing.

Kip's foster father had lied to him about buying books—and about searching for his parents. Luon was a criminal.

Edward grabbed the box of matches in his pocket, gripping them tightly so that Kip wouldn't see. He had picked them up in the Dell mansion in order to light the lamp when they went down the stairs. On the trip back to Lambsear, the brothers had almost convinced themselves they hadn't seen Luon in the mansion. It had been a trick of the light, they told themselves. But when they got to the station, Edward happened to pull the matchbox they had taken from Dell's house out of his pocket. On the back, he noticed a little picture. It was a tiny drawing of a boy, sitting reading a picture book. It was just like the ones Luon had drawn for Kip on his matchboxes at home.

While Edward and Alphonse had stood in front of the station, wondering what to do, they caught a glimpse of soldiers lining up in formation around the Bason mansion.

"I guess they're getting ready to drive off the chimeras."

"Looks like it. The attack on Dell's second laboratory will probably come tomorrow."

As they watched the soldiers lining up, Edward and Alphonse thought about Luon. Eventually, he would be captured. What would Shelley and Kip think? It had been troubling them for the whole day.

They wanted it to be a mistake. That's why they hadn't told Roy what they knew. But he had surely seen through their lie. It was only a matter of time before he found out the truth.

"Maybe he's helping Dell as a way to practice his alchemy? Or maybe the doctor's paying him well."

"Whatever his reasons are, I wish he'd stop lying. If he's got time to aid criminal activities, then he should spend a little time buying books and looking for Kip's parents, like he says he is."

Edward cared less about Luon's reasons for what he was doing and more about his betrayal of Shelley and Kip.

Now Kip was telling the brothers about the book he had been reading. "It wasn't a picture book either," he was saying. "There were a lot of hard words I had to look up. Mom said that when Luon comes home next time, she'll get him to make a desk for me to study at."

"Kip . . ." Edward reached out and put his hand on the boy's head.

"Huh? What?"

"Is Luon . . . a good guy?"

Kip was taken aback by the question for just a moment. His eyes went wide. But then, just as easily, his face broke into a grin. "He sure is!"

Edward glanced at Alphonse.

The boy was clearly devoted to Luon, but, in a few days, the report would come from the military that he had been arrested. Military reports were like that: businesslike, cold. It would be a horrible shock for Kip, no matter what Edward and Alphonse did.

All they could do was talk to Shelley first, tell her everything they knew. She would be able to help the boy understand when the time came.

Leaving Alphonse to play with Kip, Edward walked into the garden behind the bookshop.

Night had fallen completely, and stars winked in the sky. Vegetables grew thick in the garden, their lush leaves swaying gently in the breeze.

"Another night . . ." Edward muttered. The night before, when they had gone to Dell's mansion, the brothers had been elated, thinking they might be on the verge of finding a clue that would lead them back to their original bodies. Now everything seemed hopeless.

"Why does he have to lie like that?" Edward grumbled, thinking about Luon as he walked into the house.

Shelley was cooking something. He could hear the sound of steam rattling the lid of a large pot.

Edward walked into the kitchen to find her standing in front of the phone. She seemed to be lost in thought.

"Hi, we're back."

"Oh!" Shelley exclaimed, turning around in surprise. "Welcome back, Edward. Did you finish whatever you had to do?"

She smiled at him, and Edward once again found himself unsure of how to proceed.

"Yeah, that's all fine . . . Sorry, were you about to make a phone call?"

Shelley shook her head. "No, actually, I just got a call from my husband."

"What?!" Edward leaned forward. "From Luon? Why?"

A hundred thoughts raced through Edward's mind. Maybe he was giving up his life of crime? Or maybe he wanted to find out about the security at the Bason mansion.

"It was just his usual call," Shelley replied. "I told you he calls every once in a while to let me know where he is."

"Where . . . is he now?"

"In Central, it sounds like. He says he won't be home for a while. But he'll bring Kip's parents back for sure this time. Isn't that great?"

Edward stood in silence, gritting his teeth. *More lies.* Luon couldn't possibly have made it all the way to Central after being in the Dell mansion just the night before.

Shelley stood staring at the framed picture beside the phone. For the first time, Edward noticed a lonely look in her eyes.

"I wish he'd come home more often," she said, half to herself, but then she smiled. "I suppose it can't be helped."

Her quiet voice was like a knife, stabbing Edward in the heart.

His own mother, Trisha, used to look at their family picture like that, too. He had asked her once if she wanted his and Alphonse's father to come back. She had smiled and said, "I suppose it can't be helped." Just like Shelley.

But Edward knew how lonely Trisha had been. Whenever he saw her eyes fill with sadness, he promised himself he would take care of her, even though he knew the ties between a boy and his mother were different than the ties between a man and his wife—ties that no doubt connected Shelley and Luon. And those ties remained strong, even though he was away, because she believed in him.

But Luon was deceiving her, and that knowledge made Edward's stomach churn. "'It can't be helped,'" he growled. "Next time he comes home, you should just sock him one in the jaw."

"Edward, I'd never do that!" Shelley said with a laugh. She reached out to trace the edge of the photo with a finger. "Although I'd give anything for him to be close enough that I could. His voice on the phone just now . . . He didn't sound well. But I can't do anything to help. He's so far away. That's what worries me most. When I offer to help, he says no, he'll handle it himself. But I'm his wife. I want to work with him, to be with him. I want him to admit he can't do it all by himself. But he won't, and that makes me sad more than anything else."

Edward listened quietly.

"He's a good man, don't get me wrong. But he never tells me the details of what he's doing. It was the same when he gave up his last job. I know it must have been hard for him, terrible even, but he never told me why he left."

"His last job?"

"Yes. You know, he never intended to take over the bookshop. But he said that running the bookshop would let him spend more time looking for Kip's parents, so he just up and quit his old job. He used to live here with us more often when Kip was smaller, but over the past three years, he's become more serious about finding Kip's real parents, and he hardly ever comes home . . ."

Three years ago . . . That matched exactly the date on that letter from Dell. If Luon had been working as an alchemical researcher in the past, that might explain how he came to be working for Dell in the present.

"What exactly did Luon do?" Edward asked again.

Shelley frowned. "I'm sorry. He's asked me not to speak of it . . . If Kip should hear . . ."

Shelley was reluctant, but it was clear she wanted to tell someone. Edward, being a guest, made the perfect listener. There was less of a chance he might inadvertently tell Kip anything Shelley told him.

She spoke again. "His work . . . was something that Kip should never have to know."

"What do you mean?"

"You're familiar with the Ishvalan massacre?"

Edward swallowed and nodded slowly. This was entirely unexpected, but now that he thought about it, he wondered why it hadn't occurred to him before. Now he knew why Roy had taken such a particular interest in the strange man they had seen in Dell's mansion.

"He was . . . involved with the massacre. Luon was a state alchemist."

NIGHT HAD FALLEN ON LAMBSEAR, except for one corner that was lit so brightly it hurt the eyes to look at.

"Light every alleyway, every nook and cranny! There's no telling where those chimeras will come from!"

Roy's voice echoed across the Bason mansion grounds.

A high wall surrounded the large, four-story building, and the soldiers were lined up on the expansive grounds. A river ran along one side, making intrusion difficult, but Roy left nothing to chance.

He had placed guards on the entrances to the sewer system and stationed men at every street corner, in case there was a change in tactics and the chimeras came from above ground this time.

"Tell the residents on First and Second Avenues to stay inside their homes!" Roy paced across the grounds.

Havoc called out to him. He was holding a rifle, slung across his shoulder. "Hey, Colonel, we'll take on the chimeras, but what are we supposed to do if that alchemist shows his face?"

". . . I'll deal with him," Roy said after the slightest of pauses.

"Sure, but aren't you supposed to be on the brigadier general's personal guard?"

"Oh, right." Roy frowned. He wanted to be on the front lines, taking control, but Bason had specifically requested that Roy not leave his side. He was certain the man simply enjoyed ordering a state alchemist around. "Honestly, I could care less about this whole operation," Roy muttered. "If the things just want a little blood, I say we push Bason out there and let the chimeras have their fill . . ."

"Colonel," Hawkeye called out from behind him. She motioned at him with her eyes.

Roy looked around to see Bason himself come walking out of the mansion.

"You sure you'll be able to keep those chimeras out with this lot? I'm a little concerned," the massive man said, walking over, his fat swaying like a symbol of his wealth. Bason had sent an incompetent man to hinder Roy earlier in the operation, but now that it came to protecting his own skin, the team from Southern was nowhere in sight. Roy wasn't complaining—it was a relief not having to deal with them anymore—but he didn't enjoy taking orders from Bason, either.

"I'm not sure how you concocted this idea that I would be attacked next in the first place. You aren't playing games with me, are you, Colonel?"

The brigadier general had given Roy's men access to his front lawn, but apparently he still had misgivings about the operation.

Roy had been meticulous in going through all the reports of the chimera attacks, separating diversionary tactics from attacks driven by a clear purpose. When he reviewed the list of people who had actually been assaulted, all of them had their share of shady incidents in their history, and all had been involved with the military in some way.

For example, an arms merchant living near one recent attack site had been making a killing selling weapons on the black market. Another series of sightings in Dublith centered on a location the military itself had been watching for some time. The man who lived there had been involved, years before, with manipulating news on the civil war in Ishval.

During the fighting, he had taken advantage of the chaos by targeting the most able men, winning their loyalties through bribery, then trumpeting their achievements as his own.

That they had pieced these connections together so quickly was a testament to the sharp minds in the Eastern Command team as well as Roy's own considerable powers of perception. Another military unit might still have been stumbling around in the dark. Still, no charges had been brought against Bason and the others for their crimes. What made these people particularly heinous was their uncanny ability to destroy evidence, rubbing out anything that might lead to an arrest long before suspicions even turned their way.

"You've done many things in many places, Brigadier General. The one controlling those chimeras may have a grudge against you," Roy said, making up reasons as he went.

Bason didn't seem pleased. He changed the subject.

"I hear you're transferring to Central?"

"Indeed I am."

Bason smiled. "I was wondering about those chimeras who got away during that joint mission earlier. Who's taking responsibility for that again? I should think this whole thing could have been resolved some time ago if we'd gotten some leads on the chimeras back then, don't you?"

Bason's plan was clear. He had tried to foil Roy's strategy from the beginning by sending an incompetent officer to "aid" him. Doubtless, when the case was wrapped up, he would somehow try to take credit for it. Roy found himself thinking even less of the brigadier general than he had before, but he wasn't going to give the man the satisfaction of telling him that.

"I entirely agree with you, sir. I regret it deeply, in fact. If we had been able to take one of the chimeras alive, we might be getting somewhere with this investigation . . ." Roy looked up at the sky and heaved a deep sigh. "There wasn't much we could do though, after that munitions warehouse blew, taking the chimeras with it. Actually, I have to thank you for sending that stalwart officer with his team of fresh recruits. Thanks to their heroic efforts, we were able to contain the damage to only one of the munitions warehouses."

Which was Roy's way of telling Bason he knew who was *really* responsible for prolonging this investigation.

Bason fell into a gloomy silence, and Roy grinned. "I can't help but feeling," he said, "that you've never been terribly impressed with my work, Brigadier General. If it bothers you to have me on your personal guard detail, feel free to wait inside the mansion for the chimeras to come—alone."

Bason's face went pale. "No, no, that won't do. What if they got in there somehow?"

"Oh, I'll send my men right away. They're all fresh recruits, eager for combat. I'm sure they'll do you right," Roy assured him. A few other choice things he might say had occurred to Roy by this point, but he could hear Havoc behind him, trying to contain his laughter, and he could see Hawkeye staring holes in his forehead, so he decided to leave it at that. "You should be getting back inside, sir," he said politely, ushering Bason back into the mansion.

When the door had shut behind Bason, Havoc finally burst out with a guffaw. "Did you see his face? Ah, I knew there was a reason I hadn't transferred out of your command, Colonel." Havoc doubled over with laughter.

"I think you went a little far," Hawkeye cautioned, but Roy merely shrugged.

"You can't hide the facts. And if I'm going to Central, I better learn how to deal with his type. There's enough of them there, for sure."

"I'm a little worried about your future, sir," Havoc said with mock concern.

"You're not the only one. But I have to go to Central . . . and I'm not letting anyone get in my way."

Just then, a guard on top of the main building began shouting.

"They're here! On the mountain across the river!"

Whistles began to blow. Soldiers readied their weapons.

Roy quickly ran up to the wall running alongside the river, climbed up a small ladder to the top of the wall, and scanned the far bank.

Two chimeras were prowling on the train tracks that ran at the foot of the mountain. They were in plain sight, not even attempting to hide.

"How do you think they plan on getting across?" The bridges on First and Second Avenues were completely blockaded. Anything attempting to cross would make an easy target.

Raising his hand to signal his men to hold their fire, Roy watched the chimeras.

These chimeras looked like wolves, and unlike the ones they had faced by the Dell mansion, they seemed intelligent. They were large too, each more than eight feet from nose to tail.

"It might be a feint . . . which means the real attack will come from another direction . . ." Roy turned to one of the guards, when he felt something against his cheek, like an electric shock cutting through the air.

"Incoming!"

An impossibly bright light shot across the mansion grounds. While the soldiers held their breath, the ground opened up beneath them. The dislocated earth formed a wall that rose in a circle around the hole as it grew wider.

"Alchemy!" Roy grimaced.

Their opponent had snuck into the sewer systems, getting as close as possible without being discovered, then cut a tunnel with alchemy to come up straight beneath the mansion grounds.

Roy watched as five chimeras came leaping out of the hole. The soldiers surrounded the chimeras, but they couldn't use their guns for fear of hitting their companions on the other side. Roy moved quickly to reorganize the men when he caught a glimpse of another alchemical flare from the corner of his eye.

This time, the light arced across the river, drawing several large rocks up from the river bottom and suspending them, floating, above the water. Moments later, one of the chimeras on the far bank began to cross, leaping from stone to stone. When it reached the last stone, the chimera made a giant lunge over the mansion wall and landed clinging to the second story of the main building. The whole building shook with the force of the impact, and a scream came from within.

"Yeeeargh! Mustaaaaang!"

Roy stopped for a moment to determine that Bason's voice was coming from a different part of the house than where the chimera was now scrabbling to break through the wall. Then, he held up a gloved hand and rubbed his fingers together. A flame flared between his fingertips and shot toward the creature.

"Get down from there!"

An explosion burst between the chimera and the wall of the building, and the creature fell, limbs scraping futilely at the air. The chimera hit the ground hard, shattering part of the exterior wall.

Roy took careful aim and blasted it with a jet of flame before running over to peer through the crack it had opened in the wall. "There was another one out there . . ."

Nothing was moving on the far riverbank.

"Where did it go?"

Roy was about to jump down when he stopped and looked behind him. The five chimeras that had been running wild through the grounds were now trying to barge their way into the mansion. But Havoc, Breda, and the other soldiers had worked out a formation where they could take turns firing on the chimeras, and they were keeping the creatures at bay, slowly knocking them down, one by one. The soldiers knew about the regenerative properties of the chimeras' augmented blood, so Hawkeye had them shooting the things until they no longer moved, then shooting them some more for good measure.

Leaving his men to deal with them, Roy jumped down to the river bank to search for the last chimera.

He had no idea whether the creature had retreated or crossed over to his side, so he kept his eyes peeled, walking slowly until he found a large hole in the side of the bank.

"When did that get there?!"

If the chimera was trying to escape, that was fine, but if it was trying to find another way into the mansion . . .

Roy leapt through the opening and found himself in a narrow tunnel that ran into a proper waterway a little further down. The waterway was a half cylinder, with raised ledges along either side so that one could walk without stepping in the flowing channel of water.

"If my sense of direction is right, this is a ways from the mansion already," Roy said to himself. He could hear the sound of his men firing at the chimeras in the distance. He continued along, feeling his way down the dark tunnel with a hand on the wall, until he heard the ragged breathing of a beast.

"There you are!"

Flame leapt from Roy's fingertips. The flame quickly coalesced into a burning sphere and flew forward like a bottle rocket running down a wire. However, just before the ball of flame hit its mark, a wall of water rose from the tunnel floor. Roy's fireball smacked into the water with a loud fizzling noise. Before the flame sputtered out entirely, Roy caught a glimpse of the chimera turning to run toward an intersection in the waterway. The chimera took a right turn—which would take it directly beneath the Bason mansion.

Roy rushed up to the intersection and turned right. Ahead of him, the waterway rose slightly, and he could see light from streetlamps streaming down through a metal grate in the tunnel's ceiling. The chimera was nowhere to be seen.

Because the narrow waterways made discharging firearms dangerous, soldiers had been set to guard only their entrances, not the waterways themselves. Roy yelled up through the grate to the soldiers on the street above.

"There's a chimera heading toward Bason through this sewer! I want you to lock down the tunnel up ahead and fire when it gets there!"

"Right away, sir!"

He heard footsteps running away, then someone barking orders.

"Close off that entrance over there!"

"Get your weapons ready,"

Roy caught his breath. "Hopefully, that will hold it for a bit," he muttered. It had better. Roy had more pressing business to attend to. The person who made the wall of water that blocked his fireball would still be nearby.

But how to find him?

Then Roy's nose caught a scent mingling with the damp air of the sewers—the smell of faintly sweet tobacco tinged with a hint of sulfur.

Roy remembered the man who had smoked cigarettes like that, back when they fought together at the massacre at Ishval.

Red smoke hanging over the battlefield. Dust. Screams. Battle cries. Gunshots.

It was the kind of scene that could drive men mad, but one officer had made it his mission to keep his men on their feet and in their right minds. He had comforted Roy, who had been paralyzed with anguish at having to use his fire to harm people. He had patted an exhausted Hughes on the shoulder, telling him he was doing good work. He had stood up for Armstrong when he caught grief from the others for being sent back to Central and out of combat.

"You know, since you like to smoke so much, sir, you should really take advantage of our human lighter," Hughes had told him once, pointing over at Roy.

Their officer had smiled and shook his head. "The tobacco wouldn't taste half as good if I let him light it." Then he pulled out another match and lit one of those sweet-smelling cigarettes of his.

That same sweet smell now drifted through the air over Roy's shoulder. He turned around slowly. Someone was standing at the intersection behind him.

". . . Colonel Egger?"

Luon stood leaning against the wall of the waterway, his arms crossed over his chest, his face in profile looking exactly the same as it always had. The same, slender cigarette dangling between his fingers.

"Long time no see, Major Mustang . . . or Colonel Mustang, I guess it is these days."

Roy and Luon faced each other in the dim light that came filtering down from the streetlamps on the road above. They could have been back in Ishval. So little had either of the men changed since then. Except Luon wore civilian clothes now, and this time, they weren't on the same side.

Roy knew that he couldn't simply take this man into custody—not without a fight. Luon's black shirt collar was open, revealing the alchemical circle carved into the skin of his shoulder, as always. There was no telling when he might unleash his alchemy.

Luon knew Roy's strength, too. Any closer, and he risked getting caught in a wall of fire.

The two stood, tense, old friends not daring to take a step closer to one another.

"Once I heard you were on the case, I knew you'd figure out it was me."

"Actually, one of my men likes smoking even more than you do. I'd kind of gotten used to the smell of his cigarettes, which made yours stick out even more. That, and you use matches. I can smell the sulfur. That's why you never wanted to use me as your lighter, isn't it? You like the smell of tobacco and matches."

"Did I say that?" Luon asked, shaking his head. He narrowed his eyes as his mind raced back across the years.

It occurred to Roy that Luon might be waiting for his chimera to come back. If Roy wanted to do something, he'd better do it quick.

"There was something I've been wanting to ask you if we met again," Roy said.

"What's that?"

"The people the chimeras attacked . . . They were all enemies of yours in one way or another, I gather. But you spared their lives. Why?"

If he wanted blood, why not take it all? It had struck Roy as odd since this investigation started. Then there would be no need for such meticulous attack plans, and there would be fewer witnesses to corroborate facts. It would have taken the investigation much longer to get as far as it had if, indeed, it had ever gotten anywhere.

"I don't care to see any more people die," Luon answered, still leaning against the wall.

His voice carried the weight of someone who had killed many in the past. To anyone else, it might have seemed like empty justification, but Roy had been with Luon during the massacre. He understood. It made it that much harder to accept that this man, his former partner, would dirty his hands with this business now.

"I'm sorry we had to meet again in these circumstances," Roy said with a sigh. "Not just for me. I'm sure everyone who was with us back then would feel the same."

"Back then . . ." Luon echoed, a faint smile on his lips. "How are Major Armstrong and Captain Hughes holding up?"

"The major's as good as ever. Hughes is . . ." Roy stopped, then added quietly, "He's brigadier general now, you know."

"Brigadier general?" Luon raised an eyebrow. That would make Hughes one rank higher than Roy. Luon wondered for a moment how Roy felt about that, until he saw the pained look on Roy's face and understood in an instant what it meant. "I see . . ." he sighed. "The good always die young, don't they."

"That they do."

A long silence hung between the two men.

Somewhere above them, the battle with the chimeras at the Bason mansion was reaching its climax. They could hear the sound of explosions and the screaming of chimeras.

Luon stood from the wall. "Seems like your men have stopped the last of my chimeras." He turned his back to Roy.

"Where are you going?"

"There's more research to be done."

"Colonel Egger, what . . ."

. . . *are you doing,* Roy was about to ask, but he stopped. Luon probably wouldn't tell him, and Roy already knew the answer anyway. "You know nothing good can come of that research," he said instead. "Why do you keep at it? It's not like you."

Luon stopped and turned. "Why are you here protecting someone you despise and risking yourself investigating things better left to your subordinates, Colonel?"

Luon was right. This investigation was dangerous. Roy felt stung by the reprimand implied in Luon's words. He bit his lip.

He knew all too well the risks involved with what he was doing. All his men, even Edward, had wondered why he was out on the front lines. Roy typically found investigations like this to be too much hassle and sent someone else to do it in his place. Yet this time, he had a reason for coming out, for risking his own life.

"If I don't fix this situation, I can't go to Central. There's a lot at stake," Roy said in a low voice, returning Luon's stare.

One of his superiors had called to make sure Roy was giving the chimera incident his full attention. "I think this will be a good test of your abilities, to see if you're ready to come to Central," the officer had told him.

It was pressure, plain and simple.

Being a full-fledged state alchemist, a stalwart soldier with keen foresight, the commanding officer at Eastern, and a colonel to boot, Roy was not wanting for enemies. People his own age whom he had left behind on his meteoric rise through the ranks envied him, and his superiors shifted nervously in their seats, wondering when Roy would come to take their titles away.

Conceivably, some of the people who had put Roy on this case were the very ones who didn't want him moving up to Central. Struggles between the ranks took place in the shadows, but they were no less fierce for it.

He had been given a time limit of one week. If he failed, he might never get a chance at Central again. Roy couldn't entrust the operation to anyone else.

"In-fighting between the ranks, hmm? I can't say I'm surprised to hear that, coming from you."

"Oh, it's petty, I agree. Entirely without meaning. Not to mention that even if I *do* solve this case and get my position at Central, I'll just have to deal with more of the same," Roy spat, remembering the cloying voice of the officer who had spoken to him over the telephone. "But still, I'm going to Central. I don't care how petty it is. And I don't care what I have to do to advance through the ranks." Roy's black eyes shone with an inner determination that was steady and firm. "I was there at Ishval, same as you. That's why I have to get to the top."

Roy stared directly at Luon, telling his old friend exactly what he felt. Luon lowered his eyes. There was nothing more to ask.

After the Ishvalan massacre, Luon had left the army to see what he could do as a private citizen. Roy remained, to see what he could do from inside the system. They both carried the same sin on their shoulders, only the roads they chose to carry it down were different.

Eventually, the echoing reports of gunfire stopped. Only the gentle burbling of the water remained as it flowed by their feet.

"Colonel Mustang, where are you?"

"Colonel!"

On the streets above, the men were looking for Roy. He could hear Edward and Alphonse among them.

Luon turned away and Roy called to his back. "Colonel Egger! You know it's only a matter of time before we bring you in!"

"I quit the army. I'm not your colonel anymore."

Nor am I your friend.

Roy understood then that nothing he could say would reach Luon. If Roy tried to capture him now, Luon would fight back with everything he had. And if they used their alchemy, the former state alchemist and Roy would likely do some serious collateral damage to their surroundings.

Roy stood, unable to do anything but watch his old companion disappear into the darkness of the tunnel. ⊕

CHAPTER 4

A MISTAKEN WISH

ROY WENT BACK the way he had come to find Edward standing on the riverbank.

"Quite a show, Colonel," Edward commented, glancing at the rocks still jutting out of the water and the crumbled wall above them.

When Edward and Alphonse had heard from Shelley that Luon was a state alchemist, it led them to a very chilling conclusion. But they had to check with Roy before they would know for sure.

"There you are, Colonel! What were you doing down there, anyway?" Havoc called through the crack in the wall.

"You shouldn't run off like that on your own, sir!" Breda chided beside him.

"You okay down there?" Alphonse asked, sticking his head out above the two.

"Yeah, fine," Roy called back, waving a hand. Roy gave a few quick orders to his men, and turned back to Edward.

"Seeing you here makes me think that you've come to talk about something. Or maybe you've just come to apologize for hiding the fact that you knew that alchemist at the Dell mansion?"

"What makes you think I'd do a thing like that? Besides, I wasn't sure, and you should never report anything you're not sure about," Edward retorted with a glare.

Roy chuckled. "Don't worry about it. I'm sure you had a good reason to hide it from me. Why, I hear you're even staying at that alchemist's house."

"How'd you know that?"

"I did a little checking around."

"Great. Who's the one hiding things now?" Edward stuck out his lower lip in a mock pout, but a serious look soon returned to his eyes. "So . . . you knew Luon?"

"I did. What did you want to ask me about him?"

"I'd heard that Luon had Ishvalan friends. That when the war started, he took in their child for them, but . . ."

"But?"

"He's a state alchemist, right? The state alchemists were sent in there only to fight. They were in the thick of it. If Luon promised to take Kip under his wing, that's where he did it—in the middle of a battlefield. Which means that Kip's parents are most likely . . ." To his surprise, Edward choked up, unable to say what came next. He looked over at Roy.

Roy nodded. ". . . Dead, yes."

Though it wasn't until many years after the war ended, Roy had learned that Luon did once have friends among the Ishvalans. When he had encountered Luon in the sewer, he had told Roy, "The good die young." Roy understood only then what Luon was doing there with Dell and the chimeras.

"So, does that mean . . ." Edward began, but there was no need for him to say the rest. Roy already knew what he wanted to ask.

"It's what you think, Fullmetal. The areas controlled by the alchemists were hit bad. Hardly any survivors. He saved a child, yes, which probably means he was there when the parents died. That's your answer."

Edward swallowed. "I don't think I've ever been so unhappy to find out I was right." He took a deep breath. "Great, just great." Edward recalled the letter he'd found in Luon's study. The letter wasn't a communication between a prospective author and a bookseller. When Dell said "good partner," he meant he needed a talented alchemist for an assistant, someone who shared an interest in Dell's particular line of research.

Edward was baffled at first why Luon would lie like that to Shelley and Kip, until he realized Luon *wasn't* lying. He was trying to bring Kip's parents back. But he wasn't doing it by traveling the country, buying books and looking for missing people. He wanted to use Dell's augmented blood to resurrect the boy's parents—the parents he had killed—and bring them home.

"This is too much . . ." Edward groaned, clapping a hand to his mouth. Kip's parents were gone, taken out of this world by Luon's own hand. And now the man Kip loved like a father was a criminal, on the verge of being caught and jailed—or worse.

Edward thought about the warmth he'd felt in the Egger house, the smiles on Kip's and Shelley's faces, and a stab of pain went through his heart. "So . . . is Luon trying to make it up to him, somehow?"

"I doubt it. Not anymore, at least." Roy shook his head. Most of the people who had been there at the massacre weren't qualified to "make it up" to anyone. For what they had done, there could be no atonement. That went for Roy and Luon both.

"I think right now he's simply wishing. Wishing to resurrect the flesh, to restore the lives he took. Wishing he could use this augmented blood to bring back his friends. Wishing he could bring back all the Ishvalans."

Edward, who had tried to use alchemy to bring back his own mother, understood how Luon felt all too well. "What if it had been me?" he muttered to himself. "What if I had hurt others to get what I wanted . . . What would I be wishing for?"

If he'd wanted his mother back badly enough, the end would justify any means, any cost.

Roy shook his head firmly. "Don't even think that. You wouldn't hurt anyone, I know that. Your conscience is clean. You made the right choice."

Edward's eyes went wide. He hadn't expected to hear anything like that, especially not from Roy. He knew he had been wrong to attempt the forbidden art of human transmutation. It backfired, and he had lost part of himself because of it. Roy was telling him that it was okay, as long as he hadn't hurt anyone else. That saved him.

"Am I wrong? I don't see anyone around you looking particularly sad, at least."

"No, well, maybe you have a point," Edward admitted. If he had been willing to sacrifice someone else to get what he wanted, he felt certain he would have left a trail of misery behind him that left everyone he knew with nothing but sadness and pain.

"I'm sure if I had hurt anyone, you would have arrested me by now, Colonel."

"You know it. That's my job, after all. But . . ."

Roy fell silent. He had discovered something back when he first became an officer. The higher in rank you rose, the more of yourself you had to suppress, to keep hidden. He hadn't told anybody about the fierce fighting between the ranks at Central—a struggle which he was very much a part of—because he didn't want to make the lives of his subordinates any more difficult than they had to be. Roy had to move forward, unerringly, occasionally supporting his men when they faltered, and keep standing, no matter what. It was for this same reason that Luon had never told anyone what had happened to his friends at the time of the massacre. Now that he was a colonel, Roy simply carried out his missions, both for his subordinates and for himself.

"They're using chimeras to attack people and take their blood. It's a crime, plain and simple. We'll soon learn the location of their second laboratory, arrest Dr. Dell and Colonel Egger, and put this case to bed once and for all," Roy said, his voice cold and crisp. He looked at Edward. "And . . . I want your help. Please."

"My help?"

"I'm afraid Luon won't give up. He'll fight to the bitter end. And if a former state alchemist comes at me with everything he's got, well, I might have to do something I know I'd regret." Roy had seen Luon's determination when he had turned his back on him in the sewers. He took a deep breath before continuing. "I want to avoid that if I can. That's why I need you to stop Colonel Egger."

"Aren't you really the man for that job, Colonel? I mean, you've both been through the same things. You understand each other, don't you?"

"We do, and that's why I can't be the one to do it."

Edward sensed a faint tone of anguish in Roy's voice.

"You're the only person who can stand up to him. You're the only one who can look him in the eye and tell him he's wrong."

Edward had never seen Roy reveal anything so personal. Normally, if a criminal resisted, then to protect his soldiers above all else, Roy would surely take his life. That Roy would bring Edward in to ensure that didn't happen this time gave Edward a startling glimpse at the man behind the uniform.

Edward looked up at the brightening sky. It was all connected: the scars the state alchemists had left in Ishval, Luon trying to resurrect Kip's parents, Shelley and Kip still believing in him, and Roy, bearing the same pain as Luon yet choosing to stay in the military. They were all bound by the same painful ties.

"If Luon is arrested, Shelley and Kip will learn the truth. It might rip their family apart. But . . . if he survives, there's always the chance to start again," Edward said, trying to make himself believe his own words.

His own mother had waited years for a father who never came back. She didn't weep and moan, but she yearned terribly. Edward hated his father, but if he could have brought him back, Edward would not have hesitated, if only so his mother could see him one more time.

In Edward's mind, Shelley's lonely profile and Kip's smiling face overlapped with his memories of his mother.

"Leave it to me, Colonel," he said at last. Edward knew it had to be him. He was the only one who wasn't part of the circle of sadness, who wasn't tied to their grief. "Luon has to come home. I'll make him. I'll drag him back kicking and screaming to Shelley and Kip if I have to."

THE SUN WAS HIGH IN THE SKY, and the trouble at the Bason residence a faded memory by the time Kip sat down on the floor of the study at the Egger house. Tears glistened in his eyes.

"Kip? Where are you?"

Shelley called again from below, but Kip didn't answer. He wanted to be alone.

"I'll never meet my real mom or my real dad again . . . " he whispered, his head hanging. That morning, Kip had gone to meet with a person who said she knew Kip's parents. He had just come home.

He'd wanted Edward and Alphonse to come with him, but after they had run out of the house in a hurry the night before and not returned, he'd decided to go by himself. It had been a mistake. The story he heard down by the riverbank was cruel and sad, and it tore him apart.

"Your parents died in the massacre," the woman told him. She had come all the way from the next town over to see if he might not be the child of a couple she had known. He was.

When the situation grew worse in Ishval, she told him, his parents had tried to flee the country. But his mother had fallen ill with a fever, and while she was recovering, the entire Ishvalan region was closed off from the outside world. No one was allowed to leave. His parents had gone with this woman to hide in a remote area she knew of. Eventually, she had moved on, but she learned that the state alchemists had later come to the place where Kip's parents still hid. Not a single person had survived.

"It's a miracle that you lived," the woman told him. "I'm so glad, so glad. Your parents must have protected you to the end."

His heart low in his chest, Kip pulled a picture book off the shelf.

The book was well worn. It was not for lending—Luon and Shelley had bought it for Kip. Whenever Luon was home, he would sit by Kip's pillow and read it to him. When he finished, he would always tell him that one day his real father would sit and read that same book to him.

Kip believed him, and he wanted to see his real parents again very much. They were alive, they had to be. Why else would Luon not want him to call him "Dad"?

But it wasn't true. His parents were gone. He had been too young to know them when they were alive, and now he never would.

Kip rubbed his teary eyes with the palm of his hand. "I have to tell Luon," he sniffled. Luon was still out there, looking for his real parents. He had to tell him to stop, that he'd never find them.

Maybe Luon would stay at home more then. Shelley would be happy, and so would Kip. Kip thought about the three of them together, all the time, and he almost felt like he could smile again.

He had always been told that this wasn't his real family, just a temporary one until his parents returned. But maybe now he, Shelley, and Luon could be a real family.

Kip was still quite young, and slowly, his joy surged, replacing the tears. He may have lost his true parents, but he wasn't alone. Kip stood, the picture book in his hand.

He would tell Luon. And this time, he would call him "Dad." To think that his favorite person in the world, Luon, would become his father made Kip too happy for words.

"I have to go tell him!"

Kip ran down the stairs, picture book still in hand. He would tell Shelley everything, and together they would go find Luon.

But when he reached the bottom stair, Kip stopped.

Edward had come back while he was upstairs. Kip could hear him talking to someone. Snatches of their conversation drifted down the hall.

" . . . bring Luon back. I'm afraid he'll probably . . ."

"Then I'll just wait longer," he heard Shelley reply. "I've done it enough before. I can do it now. It was worse not knowing anything."

Shelley's voice was trembling. It almost sounded like she was crying.

"Where's Kip?" came another voice. "He said something about going to talk with a person about his parents today . . . Has he already gone? I wonder what they told him . . ."

It was Alphonse. He sounded worried.

"I called for him just now, but there was no answer," Shelley told him. "Perhaps he's back at the shop?"

"I think it's better if he heard the truth straight from you, Shelley," Edward said.

"Yes, you're right. I'll talk to him once I've got myself in order."

Kip held his breath, straining to hear every word. Shelley sounded sadder than he had ever heard her sound before.

"Right. I think we'll leave without talking to him, if that's okay," Edward said after a moment of silence.

"Are you okay, Shelley?" Alphonse asked. "Do you need company?"

"No, I'm fine," she replied. "Just go, go bring him home. Please."

Somehow, with a child's intuition, Kip sensed it wouldn't be good to step out and talk to them now. He didn't understand everything they were saying, but he knew Shelley was very sad about something.

Maybe now's not such a good time to tell Mom.

Kip decided he would go talk to Luon without her. Luon would know what to say to make Shelley feel better. Besides, he couldn't wait to call him "Dad." And he had just heard Edward talking about going to meet him. If he followed Edward, that would lead him right to Luon.

"We'll bring him back, promise. Let's go, Al!"

"Right. Bye, Shelley."

Edward and Alphonse cut across the small garden and headed out. Kip watched from the window, and when he was sure no one was looking, he slipped out after them.

LUON EGGER was twenty-two when he became a state alchemist.

He had already graduated from officers' school and was working in the military the day he received his official designation as an alchemist. Immediately after the ceremony, he had gone straight back to work.

He was investigating a case one day when he heard the sounds of gunfire in the distance. The screams and shouts that followed were like nothing he had ever heard. Luon rushed in the direction of the firing.

When he arrived at the scene, there were already too many people there for him to get a clear view, but he did catch a glimpse of a child lying bleeding on the ground. The boy was Ishvalan.

"He killed him!" someone was shouting. "That soldier shot that poor kid! That Ishvalan kid!"

"What?!"

There had been friction between the government and the Ishvalans on differing religious views, but it had never come to violence before. If a government soldier really had shot this child, that would make the tension all the worse. Luon grabbed a military police officer watching nearby.

"Who shot? Who shot the kid?!"

"I-I don't know!" the officer stammered. "But I think they're right. I think it was one of us!"

"We have to get this crowd under control!"

Rage had spread like a wildfire through the streets. Already, some hotheaded youths had started a fistfight in the square, and Luon heard the sound of glass breaking in the distance.

Then, an Ishvalan nearby started shouting at the officer, and others quickly joined in. Spooked by the crowd, another military police officer standing close by raised his rifle.

"Idiot, never point your weapon at civilians!" Luon jumped over, pushing the man's rifle down, but the gleam of the barrel in that one moment had been enough to catch the crowd's eye. The mob had leapt, and Luon was pummeled and beaten until he lost consciousness and everything faded to black.

When he opened his eyes, his entire body throbbed with pain. A single young Ishvalan man was standing in front of him.

Luon instinctively curled into a ball, fearing more blows, but the man did not raise his hand.

"You had yourself a rough time. Are you all right?" the man asked, helping Luon sit up. Luon looked around to find he was in an alleyway, a short distance from the square where the boy had been shot.

"I'm sorry about what they did to you. I thought I should move you away from there. It was too dangerous."

So the man had saved his life.

Apparently, the unrest had quieted down. The angry rioters were nowhere to be seen, and the town's streets had fallen silent. Despite the seeming stillness, Luon was certain that the local military headquarters would be in chaos. They would have to check for civilian casualties in the rioting and get those wounded officers to a hospital.

"Thank you," Luon said at last as he tried to stand. A trickle of blood ran down his cheek from his temple.

"Wait," the man said, pulling a bandage from his pocket and putting it over the wound. "It's not much, but it's better than nothing. Wouldn't want any blood getting on that nice watch of yours." He nodded at the silver watch in Luon's breast pocket. "So you're a state alchemist? You're working to make our country a better place, yes? I wish you luck." The man smiled and patted Luon's pocket with his hand.

From that day on, Luon and the man remained close friends.

After the Ishvalan child had been shot, riots flared up with increasing regularity, and the world around them became dangerous, but still the two men maintained ties. They would have dinner and talk about their lives, sometimes drinking until dawn. Luon offered the man dating advice, and when his own father died, the Ishvalan had comforted him. Sometimes they would just sit together and play cards for hours.

Soon they were best friends, and before they knew it, seven years had passed.

"You've moved up, haven't you, Luon? You're what, a lieutenant colonel now? Soon you'll be colonel!"

It was a sign of the times that the places where they could be seen together drinking and chatting had grown fewer and fewer. Luon and his friend found themselves outside more often than in, often sitting on a high hill where they talked and watched the stars.

"The people above me keep dying off, so I get pushed up through the ranks is all. Sometimes I think they're just giving me promotions so they can send me off to die too," Luon said grimly.

"Is that how it works? I'm happy to see you do well for yourself, but try not to die, okay?"

"Hey, I'm the last person that wants me to die. Not after I just got married last year."

"That's right! What was her name again? Shelley? You must bring her to meet me next time."

"And don't forget, you still have to introduce me to your newborn son!"

"Ah, yes, Kip. He can barely open his eyes, but when I come home and touch him on the head, even if he's sleeping, he grabs my finger in his tiny hand. I think he knows when his father is near."

"Aw, now you're making me feel all warm and sentimental."

Luon's friend smiled. "I hope he becomes a good boy, with a pure heart. These are difficult times, and I think the most important thing for us is to be kind to others." His friend laughed, a clear, bright sound in the night air.

Several days later, the Ishvalan attack plans were formed. Luon found himself promoted to colonel and ordered out to the front lines.

When his friend called him just before the invasion was to take place, he warned him to leave the country immediately. It was too dangerous for his wife and child to remain any longer. He vowed that they would meet again when the civil war had ended.

Perhaps it would have been better for him to resign as state alchemist on the spot. But most of the state alchemists remained, including Luon. Some of them believed they would only be fighting armed resistance. Others went because they felt they could identify the innocents and let them go free. Others believed that orders were orders, to be followed no matter what. Still others hoped this would end the war in their country, that this would bring peace. All of the state alchemists who went into that battlefield had their reasons.

But if they had known what they would see there, many of them surely would have quit on the spot. It was impossible to tell who was armed and who wasn't. They were too busy trying to save their own lives to worry about the lives of others. They saw their comrades fall, one after another, and for each of them who died, ten Ishvalans joined them. Their reasons and excuses for fighting became meaningless. Before long, all they cared about was protecting themselves and their men and trying to complete their mission so the madness would end.

They blocked off entire regions with giant walls made by alchemy. Then, the alchemists would attack, or soldiers with guns would rain down bullets on the people trapped inside. This happened over and over again.

When the massacre was finished, and Luon had finished cleaning up the sector for which he was responsible, he entered the killing grounds to look for survivors. Luon had managed to preserve his sanity by willfully numbing his emotions, and it had worked, until, there among the wreckage and the bodies, he heard the sound of a small child crying.

Luon looked to the great wall he had constructed. There at its base lay two forms—Ishvalans who, after trying to escape, had been shot down where they stood. The crying came from beneath their bodies.

"Colonel . . ." a soldier beside him said, his voice cracking.

"Dismissed, soldier," Luon had said. Later, he couldn't remember whether he had given the order to save the child or simply because he couldn't bring himself to order a young soldier to shoot one.

Luon went to move the bodies aside when he suddenly froze. Even though his face was caked with dried blood, he recognized his friend.

And beneath his friend's cold arm was his son, a wailing infant not even one year old, gripping his father's finger in his tiny hand.

"WORKING TO MAKE our country a better place . . ."

Luon sat with his hand touching the folded uniform on his desk, his friend's words echoing in his head. No silver watch now rested in the pocket his friend had patted so long ago. His uniform was covered with dark stains. Luon sat alone on the third floor of the new laboratory, in a little room he kept for himself.

"And now look what I'm doing," he muttered wryly. "It's enough to make you laugh . . . or weep."

The dark stains on his uniform were blood—his friend's blood.

Unable even to give his friend and his wife a proper burial on that battlefield, he had collected as much of them as he could carry, and when the remains had turned to bone, he buried them on that hill where he and his friend had spent so many evenings looking at the stars. But, so he would not forget, he had taken a fragment of bone from each of Kip's parents and put them in a small urn which he kept with his uniform.

Luon had been trying to resurrect his friend from that fragment using Dell's augmented blood.

In the middle of the flasks scattered around his laboratory, a large alchemical circle had been drawn. At its center sat an incubation vat. Occasionally, air bubbles would rise through the red liquid that filled the incubator, floating up to disappear near the top. White bone shaven from the fragment in the urn sat at the bottom of the vat, a piece of something fleshy growing from it. Luon stared at it for a long time.

He could cause flesh to grow from the bone, but it never took on a human form. When he used alchemy to combine the bone with augmented blood, the bone warped and crumbled, and the incubator would melt, glass and all. He tried changing the structural formulas and used blood freshly taken from his own body, but nothing seemed to work.

Outside, the afternoon sun soaked the town, but he had drawn the armored shutters on his windows, leaving it dark and gloomy in the laboratory—as dark and gloomy as he felt his chances for success were.

Luon touched his forehead to the incubation vat, screwed his eyes shut, and spoke to his friend as he had many times before.

"You'd be so proud of Kip," he whispered. "He's a gentle boy, just like you'd hoped. Come back. Please, come back . . ."

In the corner of his laboratory sat a copy of *The Evolution of the Body*. It had been many years since Luon first read the book. He remembered his first impression being one of disgust at the techniques it described. Yet he had read it again and again, and finally, he contacted its author, all because of Kip.

At first, when he brought Kip back from that battlefield, all the boy did was cry and reach out with his tiny fingers— but not once did he grasp hold of Luon's hand. It might have simply been a reaction to the shock of a new environment. But to Luon, it seemed that Kip knew his real father's hand.

He intended to tell Shelley what he had done someday, but once he had decided to resurrect the boy's parents, he kept silent. Using book buying as an excuse, he devoted himself to his research. Of course, Luon knew the dangers involved with this field of study, though he might not have felt as strongly about it as Roy or Edward.

Dell's augmented blood was extremely powerful, both in the speed of the regeneration it promoted and the energy it imparted on the cells it touched. Of the chimeras they had made using the blood, over seventy percent were consumed by it and ran wild. Luon then shifted his focus to using external stimulation to promote regeneration. He would no longer risk direct contact between the blood and the cells. He was well aware of the inherent instability of his materials.

All his misgivings seemed insignificant when he thought of Kip, waiting for his parents to come home.

Luon renewed his promise to the thing in the incubator that would one day be his friend—and to Kip as well, far from him in Lambsear.

"I'll bring you home, I promise," he whispered, when he heard the sound of a cane tapping up the stairs.

"Egger? Egger!"

Dell appeared at the doorway to Luon's lab.

"Look at this!" he cried, his voice shrill with excitement. "I've made a new strain of blood, and its regenerative powers are extraordinary! I rubbed it on a small cut, and it closed before my eyes! This is what we've been looking for: a true restorative!" Dell swung the flask of red liquid in his hand through the air and cackled with delight. "Who needs medicine or surgery? Outdated, antiquated tools of a dying trade! Mark my words: once the academy learns what we've created here, they'll regret having ever driven me out!"

Luon took the flask from Dell and poured a few drops upon a glass plate, then slid the plate beneath a microscope and began to examine it. He placed a chipped chimera tooth that had been sitting on the table in the liquid and gasped as the blood quickly mended the shattered fragment. Within moments, the tooth was whole, yet there was no sign of any telltale adhesion between the blood and the bone.

"Well, isn't it wonderful? This isn't like any of the augmented blood we've made before. There's no unpredictability with this batch! I'm making more of it down at my laboratory as we speak." Dell smiled. "With this, we can mend injuries, heal diseases through transfusions, regenerate entire bodies . . . Further tests are required!"

Luon shook his head. "It's still too early to say for sure. And you're dealing with such a small quantity. What will happen with a larger volume of the stuff?"

"You would have me slow down my pace? 'Proceed with caution'?" Dell glared at Luon. "And what are you doing, trying to restore your friend there in the vat? Waste your time on such diversions, and this research will never progress, your friend will never return. So don't tell me how to do my . . ."

The sound of a chimera howling from the floor below distracted Dell midsentence.

"What's gotten into him?" he said with a frown.

The next moment, all the chimeras in the garage on the first floor began to howl in unison.

Luon ran over to the window and peered out through a crack in the armored blinds.

Their factory hideout stood in the middle of town, with a good view of the deserted, dilapidated town center. Beyond the swirling dust of the streets, low hills rose in a circle around the town. Luon narrowed his eyes. He could make out a handful of men in uniforms, marching their way toward them through the hills.

"So they sniffed us out already . . ."

Luon had known it was only a matter of time, yet he hadn't expected Roy to come quite this quickly. Inwardly, he cursed his former subordinate's competence.

"What, the army again? Damn them! They've interfered with me far too much! Egger, you have to stop them!" Dell lifted his cane and swatted the wall in anger, shouting as he ran toward the stairs. "My current batch of augmented blood will be done momentarily! You know I can't move until it's finished, so you'll have to buy us time! We'll leave as soon as the experiment is complete." The old man caught his breath and cackled. "Fools! They'll never stop me! I'll just make laboratory number three and continue my research!"

Dell turned to go down the stairs, when he stopped and looked back at Luon. "Once we finish this augmented blood, you'll have what you need to bring back your friend. This is no time for doubts. Stop them with everything you've got! Understand?"

"I understand."

The old man's mouth curled upward in a satisfied smile, then he turned and scampered down the stairs, forgetting his age in his excitement. Luon returned to the window to get a better look at what the army had sent for them.

"It doesn't look like they're ready to make their move yet . . . but it will come soon enough."

They had stopped in the hills, biding their time, no doubt, because they were wary of the chimeras. This probably also meant they had brought enough weaponry with them to deal with the chimeras when the time came.

Luon pulled the plug on his incubator, temporarily suspending his experiment, and extracted the contents of the vat. He placed his old uniform and the urn with the bone fragments together in a sturdy box. He didn't want to risk them being destroyed should the factory fall down around them once the fighting started.

"I'll see you soon," he whispered, giving the box a pat, and then Luon leapt into action.

Running down to the ground floor, he made his way toward the garage, where he could hear the chimeras howling, and pressed a switch on the side of the door.

The garage shutter slowly rolled up from the ground, letting in yellow sand and light from the outside. Giant, winged reptilian things and creatures like warthogs that stood on two legs scraped at the garage door with long claws. These chimeras were wild and violent, and when the shutter rose high enough, they burst out as one into the deserted town streets.

Luon didn't wait to watch them. He ran to the rooftop, from which he could observe the soldiers as they engaged the chimeras.

"Cannons . . . and marksmen too . . . Quite a few, from the look of it," he muttered, making a mental note of what he saw.

The chimeras here at their second laboratory had even greater regenerative powers than the ones at the Dell mansion. They would be hard to take down. But the soldiers under Roy's command moved in tight formation and fought with impressive accuracy and coordination. The sound of gunshots and the roaring of the chimeras echoed through the streets, and a great dust cloud rose around the combatants.

"Chimeras alone won't be enough against Mustang," Luon said with a sigh as he steeled himself for the fight he knew would come. Dell was right: he would have to hit back with everything he had. If he bought the doctor a little time, they could both escape with the augmented blood. The chance of restoring his friend was worth the risk—worth any risk.

Luon turned, prepared to face the soldiers, and descended the steel staircase.

His footsteps echoed through the empty factory as he made his way past the fifth and fourth floors when the wall to his side suddenly warped, forming into a column of concrete that shot up in front of his eyes.

Luon hurled himself to the floor to avoid the shooting wall when he saw another wall rising in front of him, blocking his path down the stairs.

"Sorry, you're not getting out that way," a high voice rang across the empty floor.

Luon twisted around to see two figures standing a short distance away.

"Who are—"

"Edward Elric," said the shorter of the two. "I've come to stop you."

"You're not going down those stairs!" said the one in armor next to him.

Luon raised an eyebrow slightly. "Edward Elric? I've heard of you. Something about a kid genius who made state alchemist at only twelve years old. So that was you."

He had seemed young when Luon saved him at the Dell mansion, but Luon had supposed that it had partly been a trick of the light. Now he could plainly see that Edward was just a boy. Luon had heard about Edward's travels with his brother, Alphonse—most likely the one in armor standing next to him now.

The blinds on that level were open, and sunlight stabbed through the windows, lighting the factory floor. Wooden boxes and various pieces of furniture left by the former occupants cast pools of shadow where they lay scattered around. In the middle of this stood Edward and Alphonse, facing him.

"Sorry, Luon, but you're coming with us," Edward said, tensing, his eyes locked with those of the former state alchemist. Edward wanted nothing more than to charge in, tie Luon up, and take him back right away, but if he made a mistake and Luon escaped, all their effort finding this place would have been in vain. Nor could he let Luon take the fight outside. A well-armed squad was waiting for him, and odds were good that he'd be shot out there. Edward wasn't going to let that happen. He had promised to bring Luon back to Shelley and Kip, so that's what he would do.

"Luon," Edward called out across the factory floor. "I know about your loss, and I know it's been hard for you. But what you're doing here is wrong."

"You really think your friend would want you to hurt so many people just to bring him back?" Alphonse asked.

Luon looked at the two boys standing there resolutely, and his face twisted with the hint of a smile.

"Who are you to tell me that I'm wrong? How do you know what my friend would want?" His smile fading, Luon glared at Edward and his brother. "He left behind his only son in this world. You think he wanted to die? What if he *wants* to come back, to see his child again? What about everyone else who died? Wouldn't they want to come back? To have back the lives that were taken away from them? No one can know what the dead want. Least of all you."

Luon grunted and raised his hand, preparing to use his alchemy to punch a hole in the wall Edward had created across the stairs.

Edward moved quickly. Slapping his hands together and then touching the floor, he sent a lump of stone rising up from the floor by Luon's feet.

Luon staggered back, dodging the stone pillar that only narrowly missed his jaw. "Get out of my way!" he shouted.

"I said you're not leaving unless it's with us!" Edward shouted back. "There's nothing for you here, Luon. Can't you see that? Even if you could restore his flesh, it doesn't mean what you create will be your friend! How are you going to recreate his mind? Or his soul?"

Alchemy described the human body as comprising three parts: the flesh, the soul, and the spirit. If you restored the flesh without considering the other two, you would have nothing but a mindless lump of tissue.

"Empty theories!" Luon spat back. "No one knows which of the three comes into this world first. If you create the flesh, why wouldn't the spirit and the soul come back to dwell within it?"

Edward shook his head. "Why can't you get your mind off the dead and start thinking a little bit about the living? What about paying attention to Shelley and Kip for a change?"

"Shelley . . . and Kip?" Luon's eyes went wide at the mention of the two names.

"We've been staying at your house, you know!" Alphonse said from where he stood a few paces behind his brother. "You should hear Kip talk about you. He loves you, Luon! Stop this, please! Kip wants you to come home. He's waiting for you!"

Luon lowered his eyes, but a moment later his face lifted again. "I've been wrong to Shelley, I admit that. But Kip isn't waiting for me. He's waiting for his real father!"

No sooner had the words left his mouth than Luon reached for the pillar of stone Edward had made by his feet. Alchemical light flared, and the stone lengthened into a sharp point, driving into the wall Edward had built across the stairs, piercing it through the middle. In a matter of moments, the stairs would be clear again. Edward scowled and reached down to fashion a long, spearlike weapon of his own out of part of the floor.

"Al, I'm going to drag him back into the middle of the room. You go fix that wall!"

"Got it!"

Edward ran for Luon and brought his spear down in an arc toward the man's shoulder. As he expected, Luon dodged to one side, giving Edward room to leap past him. Edward now stood between Luon and the stairs. Edward swung his spear down and held it ready in front of him. If he wanted to avoid the spear again, the only direction Luon could go was back out onto the factory floor.

Another sudden flash of light, and Edward's spear thinned, its tip shooting straight toward Luon. With no time to react to this swift display of alchemy, Luon retreated back to the middle of the room.

In the meantime, Alphonse had run behind the two and used his own alchemy to seal off the stairs firmly.

"You really are determined to stop me, aren't you?" Luon called out, ducking another jab from Edward's spear.

"And you're really determined to fight," Edward shouted back. "Well, you're in luck! I just so happen to be a state alchemist. You can warm up on me before heading out to face the army."

"Ah yes, the state alchemists. Do you have any idea what they really are, I wonder?" Luon asked, his eyes burning into Edward's. "Human weapons, capable of incredible destruction and protected by the shield of state authority. It's only a matter of time before they send you out onto the battlefield to do exactly what we did in Ishval, you know. Are you ready for that, Edward? Do you know what a terrible, horrifying thing that is?"

Edward stood facing Luon and lifted his hands, his fingers spread wide. He had never experienced a massacre, or anything even close. Although he had learned about them in school, they seemed like far and distant things. Now, having met Kip and hearing of Roy's own struggle with the past—and seeing what had become of Luon—it was clear that the wounds left by what had happened in Ishval remained fresh for those who had been there.

Power like Edward's combined with the callousness of authority could be a terrible thing indeed. Weren't there people in the world being oppressed by that very power even now? Edward thought about himself being given that strength, and it chilled him.

"It's probably worse than anything I can imagine," he said after a pause, "and yes, it frightens me. Now I only use my powers when I want to—when I think it's right, but if I had to use them against my will, to follow orders . . . to kill someone . . ." He swallowed. "It scares me to think about it."

Just the thought that he, Edward, could make an orphan of a child like Kip caused his heart to freeze with terror.

But there was no denying the power he possessed, and there was no denying he wanted that power. Edward clenched his fists and quickly glanced back at Alphonse. He needed money and information if he was ever going to see his brother's body restored. That was what made him become a state alchemist. It might not have been the noblest choice, but he had more important things to do than worry about his government's policies or its past.

"Say what you want, but we need this power!" Edward said, his voice growing stronger. "I knew what it meant when I became a state alchemist, and I'm ready to do whatever it takes to stay one."

"So, that's your answer?" Luon said sadly. A pained expression quickly passed across his face. The next instant, his hand reached back, touching a discarded metal table on the floor next to him, and light flared from his fingertips. In a flash, the table warped into a long, sharp-edged sword. Weapon in hand, he lunged for Edward.

"I have determination, too, state alchemist Elric! I'm going to bring back Kip's parents, and you're not going to stop me!"

"You're wrong!" shouted Edward, knocking aside Luon's sword with the cutting edge of his spear. "Kip is waiting for his parents, but they're gone! You're his father now! Why can't you see that? You're the one who saved him!"

Edward stepped forward, swinging his spear down at Luon's shoulder. But Luon was quicker. He dropped to his knees and touched the floor before jerking both hands upward again. A section of the floor shot up like a geyser of rock, striking Edward's spear from beneath.

"Dammit, he's fast!"

Roy had warned Edward about Luon's speed when they held their strategy meeting back in Lambsear, but seeing it firsthand was something else.

"Okay," Edward said, panting for breath. "So you've got range, speed, and accuracy . . . I'd say your alchemy's just fine." Edward let go of his spear, now hopelessly embedded in Luon's newly fashioned wall. "But how about this?!" In a blur of motion, Edward leaped over the wall and swung a tightly clenched fist at Luon's face.

The older man ducked aside by a hair and grabbed Edward by the arm in an attempt to throw him to the floor. But Edward was fresh from sparring practice in Dublith. Compared to sparring with Izumi, this was a piece of cake.

For a split second, Edward seemed to be falling toward the floor as Luon intended, but before he hit, he reached out a hand, twisted out of Luon's grasp, and swung one leg around in a well-aimed kick.

"Unnk!" Luon gasped as Edward's foot connected with his shoulder.

"That's not all!"

Straightening himself and clapping his hands together, Edward pressed his palms into the floor. Lightning raced from his fingertips, and the floor beneath them swelled. "Try this one on for size!"

A cylindrical column emerged from the floor and shot along it, cutting a trench through the concrete in a beeline for Luon. Edward was sure it would hit, but Luon slapped a hand on the wall to his side and pushed it with his arm. The wall buckled, lurching to one side and pulling the floor beneath it up before Edward's column could reach him. In the blink of an eye, a large wall had formed in front of Luon. The hurtling cylinder collided with it, and the entire factory shuddered with the force of the impact.

"Man! He's persistent!" Edward groaned under his breath.

From the sound of the gunshots outside, the army had already surrounded the building, but Luon showed no signs of surrendering. Edward had noticed the needle marks on Luon's arm when he was doing his alchemy. *He's been drawing his own blood to resurrect Kip's parents*, Edward realized, *and now he's going to face me and an entire squad of troops to boot—this guy doesn't care if he dies, does he?*

"I'm telling you, you're wrong!" Edward shouted, forming another spear out of the floor. "You think your life is yours to throw away, but there are people waiting for you, Luon! What about them? And what about all the people your chimeras have attacked?!"

"What does it matter, if I can bring Kip's parents back!" the man snarled back.

As alchemy flared and Edward and Luon ripped up pieces of the building around them to throw at each other, the floor they were on gradually deteriorated. Part of the ceiling collapsed, and the room was filled with rubble and swirling dust.

Edward, who had fashioned his right arm into a blade to fend off Luon's attacks, glanced back at Alphonse. His brother had been waiting by the wall to block Luon's escape that way, and he had just finished drawing a large alchemical circle on the wall.

Edward turned back and touched a hand to the floor. A light flared, brighter than any yet, brighter than the sun, and a wall rose up beneath his fingers. This time he dragged in not only the floor, but part of the building's wall as well, until his own wall grew so high it touched the ceiling.

"Now, Al!"

At Edward's signal, more light flared from Alphonse's hands, and a long pillar shot from the circle next to him, cutting across the floor until it hit Edward's wall. Struck by the rapidly thrusting column, the wall toppled, sending up another thick cloud of choking dust.

Luon, his view blocked by the immense wall, quickly threw up a pillar of stone to block its fall.

This was the moment Edward had been waiting for. He crossed his arms in front of his face and slammed into a section of his wall that he had made purposely thin. The wall disintegrated into fragments as Edward burst through right in front of the flailing Luon.

"Wake up!" he shouted. "There's no sense in hurting people to bring back Kip's parents! You'll never be able to take back the fact that you killed them! You need to face the truth before it's too late!" Edward clenched his fists. The air shuddered around him from the impact of alchemically transmuted concrete and metal. "The past doesn't matter! You're the only father Kip will ever have!" he shouted as he drove his fist up into Luon's solar plexus.

Luon fell just as the rest of the wall hit the floor with a thunderous boom. The shock sent cracks running through the floor, so damaged now that it could barely support its own weight.

Edward felt the floor drop out from underneath him, but he didn't fall. He looked up to see Alphonse holding onto his arm. Before their eyes, a large section of the floor shattered and collapsed down to the story below.

"Luon!"

Alphonse peered down through the billowing clouds of dust, but Luon was nowhere to be seen.

Edward, ever mindful of the conservation of matter, had been careful not to take too much of the building's structure when he made his wall—but he hadn't accounted for Luon's own attempt to keep the wall from falling. The stone buttress Luon had made was too heavy for the floor to support.

"Oh, no!" Alphonse shouted.

"It's okay," Edward said. "He's only fallen one floor, and it doesn't look like he fell far. He'll be fine—and unconscious, if we're lucky."

"I hope so. I wasn't sure how we were going to explain this one to Shelley and Kip."

Edward gave his brother a rap on the arm. "Thanks, Al. You caught me just in the nick of time."

"That's why I'm here," Alphonse replied with a chuckle. "To keep you out of trouble—or pull you out if I have to. Now let's get down there!"

"Right!"

As one, the brothers turned toward the staircase. They were just about to remove the wall blocking off the stairs when they heard a low sound echo through the building below.

"What was that? Someone's voice?"

"A chimera?"

They could still hear the sounds of the army engaging the chimeras outside.

Havoc's team had been the first to greet the chimeras when they rushed out of the laboratory, but when the creatures, with their augmented blood, refused to die, Breda's team of sharpshooters took over. First, they shot from the safety of the hills to avoid getting too close to the blood-drinkers, but once the chimeras' numbers were down, they moved in, until the factory building was completely surrounded.

It was slow going, fighting creatures that could take round after round without stopping, but gradually the circle around the laboratory tightened.

The brothers heard another roar from below. They had thought at first it was the death wail of some chimera, but they were wrong. The half-shattered wall next to them crumbled, sending stone fragments down to the floor.

The sound hadn't come from outside.

Edward and Alphonse stared down at the floor beneath their feet. It vibrated as the eerie voice echoed through the building. ✦

CHAPTER 5

KEEP MOVING ON

KIP PEERED OUT OF THE TRUCK at the low dusty hills of an unfamiliar land. Several hours had passed since he followed Edward and Alphonse to the convoy and slipped unnoticed into one of the trucks. He had been surprised to see men in military uniform—soldiers—getting into the trucks, but if going with the Elric brothers meant finding Luon, Kip was ready for anything.

The truck had swayed and rocked along bumpy roads for a long time while Kip crouched in the back. When the trucks stopped, he heard the men get out and begin shouting orders.

"Keep outside the town," he heard one man say. "I want all of squad B waiting on those hills."

"Check your gear and weapons, men," another shouted.

When he could no longer hear them talking, Kip crept outside and took cover behind a nearby bush. The trucks were parked in a circle in the middle of a barren field. He could see several soldiers on a hill in the distance.

Kip hurried away from the trucks, with all the warnings the Ishvalans down by the river had given him about the military running through his mind. On the other side of the hill, he caught sight of a town.

Maybe that's where Luon is, he thought, heading in the direction of the buildings, but when he came closer, he saw that it was unlike any town he had ever seen. There were no people, no pets, nothing moving at all.

Where is this place?

He saw crumbling houses and flower boxes with no flowers blooming in them. He had expected to find Luon the moment he jumped out of the truck, but now, faced with this deserted town, he felt uneasy. He hugged the picture book he had brought with him tight in his arms.

The soldiers were gathering on the hill in the distance. Kip crouched low so they wouldn't see him, and he began searching the town. He knew that Luon often bought books from publishers and larger bookstores, so he made for the largest building he could find: a large, abandoned factory.

Quietly opening a small door in what looked like the back side of the building, he slipped in. He found himself standing in a long hallway, dark and gloomy despite the bright sunshine outside. "Luon?" he called, his voice sounding much smaller and fainter than he had intended to sound. There was no reply. "Are you in here somewhere?"

Kip had no time to lose. He wanted to find Luon and tell him about his parents. He wanted to thank him for searching for so long. Shelley was crying. He had to get Luon to come home and comfort her. On the way back, he would take hold of Luon's hand and call him "Dad."

He walked, each step more timid than the last, when he heard a sudden sound, like dogs howling, on the other side of the corridor wall. Then came a rattling sound, like a metal shutter opening, and as he waited, holding his breath, he heard gunshots and the yowling of beasts.

Frightened, Kip turned and ran up the staircase on the other side of the hall. When he reached the second floor, he heard someone moving. Kip rushed out into a large room, hoping beyond hope he had finally found Luon.

Like the hallway below, this room was oddly dark. Glass jars filled with red liquid and steaming flasks that bubbled and boiled cluttered a table, before which stood an old man in a white lab coat.

The old man had his back to Kip, wholly engrossed in some sort of experiment. Kip watched as he paced and whirled, his long, wrinkled fingers taking pinches of powder and placing them inside one of the vials.

"Um . . ." Kip said, and the old man looked around. The way his eyes seemed to gleam in the darkened room scared Kip, but he summoned up his courage and spoke. "Excuse me, but I'm looking for someone."

"What's this, a child?" the man said quizzically. "I don't believe whomever you're looking for is here." He waved a wrinkled hand in irritation. "I've no idea how you got in here, but you must leave. I'm busy, if you couldn't tell. Damn those soldiers! I'll need to leave as soon as this test is through, and there's so much more I could be doing! Go home, you," he said again, glaring at Kip. "Or have you come to disturb my research too?"

Kip didn't understand much of what the man said, but the coldness in his voice made it clear that Kip wasn't welcome. He started to leave, when he remembered the fearful howling he had heard below and hesitated. He thought about going farther up, but something had begun slamming into the walls on one of the upper floors, and the vibrations made the building around him shudder.

This old factory was starting to become a very frightening place.

While Kip stood there shivering, the old man gazed intensely at the red liquid in one large beaker. He then set a stopwatch on the table beside it and turned around.

"What, you're still here?" He scowled, and Kip shrank back. Suddenly, the old man burst into eerie laughter. "Yes, perfect, perfect! You've come at just the right time! Perhaps you might assist me?"

The old man walked swiftly toward him with his cane and grabbed Kip by the arm. "I'll need a bit of your blood. Or maybe you'd like to be the first human test of my augmented formula, yes?" The old man cackled. "Come, come, there's nothing to be afraid of."

The old man dragged Kip, who struggled with all his might to pull away, when he noticed the brown skin on the boy's arm.

"Hrrm? An Ishvalan? Ah, I know you, you're Egger's boy!"

"You know my dad?!" For a moment, Kip forgot his fear and looked up at the old man, his eyes full of hope.

But the old man fixed him with a curious look. "Your dad? Hrrm . . . You mean the man Egger killed?"

"Huh?" For a moment, Kip didn't understand what he was saying.

Seeing the surprise on the boy's face, the man gave another whoop of laughter. "Eh? You mean to tell me you don't know? Ah, of course . . . I suppose Egger wouldn't have told you. How could he?" He cackled again. "Then I'll tell you who Egger is: he's a state alchemist, a killer of Ishvalans."

Kip had heard about the state alchemists. He knew about the massacre, too. Whenever other Ishvalans said the word "alchemist," they said it with venom on their lips or a dark shake of their heads. Some said they should drive the memory of the alchemists from their minds, while others told him to hurl rocks and insults if he should ever meet one.

But Kip himself had no reason to hate the state alchemists. After all, he knew his parents were still alive somewhere, and he was far too young to understand the magnitude of what had happened.

"Luon . . . is a state alchemist?"

"That he is, or was! And he killed your father and mother with his own hands, he did. Tee hee! Why do you think he works here with me? He's trying to make you new parents! Tee hee hee!"

The old man laughed his eerie laugh for some time before finally pushing Kip away. "Go home, boy. Egger will be home soon, with your regenerated parents behind him, I'm sure. Aha! The final test is complete!"

Kip stood a few feet away, staring into space, his lips struggling to find words.

"No . . ."

But the old man had already forgotten about his visitor. He danced a little dance in front of his laboratory table and chortled in delight. "Magnificent! The academy will see me for what I am now! How could they even think of stopping this research? I will create the perfect body, one that can mend injuries and illness from inside! Ha ha! Then they can shoot me all they want, and I'll still continue my work! Ah ha ha ha!" The old man's words trailed off, lost in his mad laughter. He drew liquid from the beaker into a large syringe and began injecting it into his own arm.

But Kip didn't see any of this.

"No . . . It's a lie . . . It has to be."

In a daze, he took one step back, then another, then turned and staggered out of the room, muttering to himself.

"It can't be true. Not Luon . . . He'd never . . . He's been looking for my real parents . . . He wouldn't kill them . . . He's lying . . ."

Then the picture book he carried—the one Luon promised that his real father would read to him—began to feel very heavy. It slid out of his hands and fell onto the floor with a soft thump.

An incredible booming sound thundered from the floor above, and chunks of the ceiling fell down around him, but Kip stood still, his eyes wide open, staring into space.

Then he heard someone calling Luon's name on the floor above. Kip reached out for his book, but instead his fingertips found a piece of rubble the size of his fist.

Grabbing the rock tightly, Kip began walking slowly up the stairs.

LUON OPENED HIS EYES and groaned. He was lying on the third floor landing, where he had fallen—along with much of the floor—after the fight with Edward. He had been unconscious for only a moment. The dust clouds kicked up by the collapse of the ceiling still swirled around him.

Luon lifted himself out of the rubble and tried to stand, but he quickly fell to his knees. He groaned. A searing pain shot through his chest. It was the same place where Edward had struck him, but his agony ran deeper than Edward's blow.

"The only father Kip will ever have . . ." Luon whispered, looking down at the floor. The thought never occurred to him before. For so long, he had believed that the only kindness he could offer Kip was to bring his real parents back—not as some kind of atonement, not to win forgiveness. He merely wanted to restore the family he had torn apart.

The one who should hug Kip was his friend, not him.

This unwavering truth was all that drove him, until Edward's words turned that truth into pain that gnawed at Luon's heart.

"What do you want me to do?" he grimaced, driving a fist into the floor.

If Luon told him everything, Kip would be devastated. Edward had said that, as long as he was alive, he could still make things right. But how could he when he had only sadness and misery to offer the boy? The thought made him hang his head in shame.

As Luon lay there, pain burning in his chest, he heard the sound of footsteps coming through the rubble. He lifted his eyes expecting to see Edward and Alphonse, but standing before him was . . .

"Kip?"

Kip was in Lambsear. He couldn't be here. For a moment, Luon was too shocked to think, but then he remembered they were in danger—the military had the building surrounded.

Luon reflexively ran toward Kip, but then he stopped short.

Kip stood motionless, a stone clenched tightly in his hand. He stared up at Luon with an unwavering gaze.

"Did you kill them, Luon?" he said, his voice lacking any warmth. "Did you kill my mom and dad?"

Luon stood frozen, unable to move or speak.

"You lied to me! You said you'd bring my real father home!" Kip shouted, hefting the stone in his hand above his head. Yet he did not throw it.

His knuckles white, his fingers clenched around the stone, Kip began to cry.

He knew in his head what the old man had said about his real parents, but he didn't know in his heart. All he knew was the Luon who held him in his arms and read him book after book whenever he came home.

He wished he could forget that. He wished he could think only of his real parents. He wished he could throw the stone.

But he couldn't do that to Luon—not kind, gentle Luon who had always cared for him.

Kip choked back a sob, unsure what to do. He just wanted someone to stop him, to hug him. He wanted a father. He glared at Luon, and tears began to stream from his eyes.

Even when the first wailing sob broke through his lips, he didn't lower his stone. But when the second sob came, he threw the stone aside and ran into Luon's arms.

"Dad!" Kip shouted at him, wrapping his arms around Luon's neck. He didn't know whether he was calling to his dead father or to Luon. It didn't matter. He just wanted to cry.

Luon's eyes burned. He could see the storm raging in Kip's heart.

He had been prepared for anything. If Kip threw the stone, he wouldn't step aside. No matter what Kip said, what Kip called him, he knew he deserved it, and he would stand and take it. But all Kip did was cry.

"I'm sorry, Kip," he said at last. "I'm so sorry!"

He didn't want forgiveness. He didn't even feel like he had a right to comfort this boy. It was all Luon could do to whisper "sorry" over and over again.

The box holding his old uniform and a part of his old friend lay on the ground by his knees. It was a sturdy box, but the impact of the fall had cracked it open.

Luon gazed down at the tiny urn and noticed it was trembling.

For the first time, Luon became aware of a little sound like the howling of wind and deep vibrations running through the floor beneath their feet, growing stronger and stronger. He looked up with a gasp to see an almost indescribable thing bearing down on them.

A creature was crawling through the rubble, its shape vaguely that of a man. Yet its gelatinous form grew with every inch, picking up pieces of rubble and chunks of stone as it came.

"Wrrrroooor!"

The creature roared. Then, to Luon's amazement, it spoke. "Tee hee hwwwor! See the power of the augmented blood? So strong! Tee hee! Look, Egger! Can you see? I can walk without my cane . . . It's perfect . . . perfect!"

The voice belonged to Balerea Dell, even though the body did not. As Luon had feared, Dell must have injected his augmented blood directly into his body. The blood had taken over, driving him completely mad.

Now Dell's cells were hungry—and growing. Something that might once have been a hand began reaching toward them.

Luon pulled Kip away from the groping tentacle, hugging him in his arms. There was no time to use his alchemy to fight back. The tentacle struck, knocking them to the floor. Luon gasped, as the impact had knocked the wind out of him, but still he held Kip firmly in his arms. Then he stood and began to run. He had to get the boy to safety.

"Run, Kip!" he shouted, but the boy wouldn't let go of Luon's neck. "Kip, you have to run," he shouted again. "I'll get Dell's attention. Please!"

"No!" Kip shouted, burying his face under Luon's arm. "No! I want to stay with you!"

Back by the river, Alphonse had told him that if he liked living with the Eggers, he should stay with them—and Kip loved Luon. He wanted to be near him, and he wanted Luon to stay. Part of Kip was afraid that, if he let go now, Luon would leave again, never to return. With his parents dead, Shelley and Luon were all he had now. He didn't want them to leave him.

"I want to stay here with you!" he shouted again.

"Kip . . ."

Sobbing, Kip hugged Luon even tighter.

Then, from behind, the tentacle reached out to them, destroying the staircase as it came. Hugging the boy tight in one arm, Luon spread his other hand on the ground. A shaft of rock with a jagged, sawlike edge shot up from the floor, slicing the tentacle in half.

The old scientist looked nothing like a human now. He roared, growing larger by the moment. His mind was entirely gone. Lost to an insatiable hunger, the creature that had been Dell flailed around with its tentacles, searching for anything to consume.

Then the tentacle lurched with amazing speed, catching Luon around the neck. Luon quickly pushed Kip behind his back. Luon worried less about getting free of the tentacle than about finding a way to keep Kip safe. His mind was racing when, right before his eyes, Dell's horrible maw opened wide.

"No!" Kip screamed by Luon's ear. The creature that had been Dell roared.

Then the tentacle around Luon's neck loosened its grip and fell to the floor, fluid streaming from its cleanly severed end.

"Show some respect! Can't you see they're having a moment here?"

It was Edward, his right arm-blade dripping with slime. He lifted his arm and cut into the mass of flesh that once was Dell's torso on the backstroke.

"Wrrrrrrorgh!"

The large cut healed with incredible speed, but apparently, the creature could still feel pain. Dell withdrew, sliding away across the rubble-strewn floor.

"You okay?" Alphonse asked, running to help Luon, who was coughing and rubbing at his throat.

"Edward! Alphonse!"

"Kip, what are you doing here?" Edward asked, shaking his head in disbelief.

"I know," Alphonse said, turning around to face Kip. "You wanted to find Luon yourself, didn't you?"

Kip nodded, smiling through his tears.

Edward scratched his head and grinned. He turned to looked down at Luon, who was just catching his breath. "I was going to keep hitting you until you started listening to me, but I see Kip here's saved me the trouble."

Luon looked up, a hint of suspicion in his eyes.

Edward reached out his hand. "I saw you save Kip's life back there. You make a great dad, you know?" Luon accepted Edward's hand and rose to his feet. Kip came and took hold of Luon's other hand.

Luon felt Kip's tiny hand in his own and realized Edward had been right all along. He was the only one Kip had to hold on to. He had been wasting time, hurting others for the sake of his research, when what he should have been doing was holding Kip and not letting go. Instead of wasting his efforts on a dream, he should have put them to good use, giving Kip the happiest life he could.

Luon gave Kip's hand a squeeze.

He could spend the rest of his life apologizing for what he'd done, but he knew there could be no forgiveness. Maybe the day would come when Kip's anger boiled over. But he would hold on to Kip's hand and do whatever he could. Like his friend who died protecting Kip on that battlefield, he would protect the tiny life he had found there with all his power. It was his duty as Kip's father.

Edward and Alphonse stood, watching the two of them holding hands for a moment before they snapped back to reality. There was a mad, monstrous scientist-thing on the loose that needed catching.

"Where did he go?" Edward scanned the room, when the entire building shook with the force of an explosion.

"Yikes!"

"What was that?"

Edward ran over to the window. Dell was on the move, slithering out of the factory toward the soldiers on the hill. The soldiers were still too busy fighting the chimeras. They'd had no time to react to this latest threat.

Dell moved quickly, reaching out his tentacles to pick up fallen chimeras and absorb them into his body like a giant amoeba. From above, his watery, amorphous form made him look like a pond that walked.

Then the big guns near the top of the hill fired, and a shell impacted near him, blowing away part of Dell along with a chunk of the factory. Knowing Edward and Alphonse were inside, Roy's men held back from a full bombardment, but the size of their adversary made collateral damage to the buildings unavoidable. The cannons fired again, and the sound filled the sky over the deserted town.

"We have to get out there and help them," Edward said, but it was Luon who moved first.

"You watch Kip," he shouted, breaking into a run.

"H-hey! Where are you going?" Edward called after him. "It's just like Shelley said, this guy doesn't tell you anything!" Edward ran down the stairs, calling back to his brother.

"Al, stay there with Kip!"

"Got it. Be careful!"

Edward waved and ran down the torn and tangled metal stairs to the floor below. When he looked over the railing, he saw Luon had almost reached the bottom. Edward grabbed the railing, leapt over, and landed by Luon's side.

Luon stopped, surprised for a moment. The two exchanged a brief glance and then began to run together, side by side.

"You've got moves, kid!"

"I know."

They cut across the first floor and into the garage, now empty of chimeras. Edward glanced over at Luon.

"Hey."

"What?"

"It looks like you made your peace with Kip . . . but don't forget about Shelley." Edward spoke in a quiet tone. "She was all smiles when she invited us to stay at the house, but I caught her looking at your picture once, and I don't think I've ever seen anyone look so sad."

If his own father had ever come home while his mother was still alive, Edward probably would have socked him one in the jaw. Still, he knew all would have been forgiven the moment his mother smiled. Of course, this was all conjecture. His mother was long dead, and his father, still missing, had never come home.

But Egger's family was different. Luon would be in for some jail time, but he would eventually come home, and the three of them could live as a family again. Edward wanted to make sure he understood how important that was.

"Don't make her cry again, okay?" Edward said with a glare at him.

Luon smiled faintly. "I won't. I promise."

Edward grinned. "Then let's get this mess cleaned up!" The two ran out of the garage.

Outside, Roy's men prepared to face Dell. Roy must have used his alchemy. Flames flickered and flared across much of Dell's massive body. But it looked like the augmented blood was already doing its work, repairing and regenerating what had been lost. The flames smoldered, spluttered, and died.

"Gyyyyyyyooooooowrr!"

Dell advanced on the hill, his body rippling and consuming everything in his path.

"That thing just keeps on repairing itself! What's happening to him? You think we'll ever get Dell out of there?" Edward asked Luon as they stood watching the creature's advance. Luon picked up a stick and quickly drew a diagram on the ground. "Dell's true body is at the center of that thing—its nucleus—and the augmented blood surrounds him, protecting his exterior. If we can get rid of the blood, we might be able to extract him from it."

"But with the blood protecting him, none of our attacks will do anything, will they?"

"No," Luon shook his head. "But the volume of augmented blood isn't all that great. If we can hold him down in one place and damage his surface somehow, then the augmented blood cells will move out from the center and attempt to repair it. Then all we'd have to do is cut them away from the rest of Dell . . . quickly."

Luon scratched a line across the outside edge of his diagram and looked up at Edward. "This is my mess, and I intend to clean it up . . . but I could sure use your help."

"Good, because I'm coming along whether you want me to or not."

The two ran past Dell, who easily stretched over one hundred feet long, until they reached the base of the hill. Luon looked back over his shoulder. Roy stood on top of the hill, ordering his troops. For a brief second, their eyes met.

"Yeeeearrrk!"

Luon wrenched his eyes back to Dell. The nearest side of him was spreading toward them and rising, blocking out the sun. If they didn't move quickly, they'd be swallowed beneath that gelatinous mass.

Luon quickly slammed a palm down on the ground. The earth swelled into a ridge that shot across the ground in a wide circle around the creature. Luon gestured, and the ridgeline rose, forming a dome above Dell. Wind swirled around them as a massive volume of earth thundered into the air.

Just when the edges of the dome were about to meet, a sharp crack rang out, and a ball of flame rose from the top of the hill. The fireball roared through the air like a rocket, falling down through the opening in the dome the moment before it sealed, enveloping everything in flame. The resulting explosion shattered the dome, exposing a giant mass of seared and steaming flesh, cooked in an instant by the superheated blast inside the dome.

"Oouuuuut ooof myyyy waaaay!" howled an unearthly voice, Dell's determination persisting even though his mind was gone. Then the creature that had been Dell roared. Just as Luon had predicted, the augmented blood rushed to the surface, trying to repair the damage. A massive tentacle spurted from the nebulous form, and Edward ran to cut it off with his arm-blade.

But his blade never reached its mark.

"This one's mine!" shouted Luon from behind him, slapping his hands down on the ground once more. A blinding light arced from his fingers, splitting the ground in a crevice that shot toward Dell, running directly under him.

"Hope that cuts you down to size!" Edward shouted. The black crevice opened wide beneath Dell, pulling down the tentacled outer shell while another protrusion of rock thrust upward from inside the crevice, launching Dell's human body into the sky.

Dell's scream echoed across the dry, barren hills, and it was over.

THE EGGER HOUSE looked much the same as always, tinged pink in the light of a beautiful sunset.

Edward walked up the sloping hill. He saw Shelley standing in the street by her house, gazing down at the sparkling river below and called out to her.

"Shelley!"

She looked up. Edward pointed a thumb back over his shoulder.

"I brought someone for you, as promised."

Just behind him, Luon and Alphonse walked up the slope with Kip between them, holding onto their hands.

Shelley's lip trembled. She looked as if she might cry, but she held back the tears.

"Mom!" Kip let go of Alphonse's and Luon's hands and came running toward her. "Luon's back, Mom! He has to leave again real soon . . . but Edward brought him back so that he could see you first!"

"Kip! There you are! I was so worried," Shelley said, hugging the boy as he ran into her arms.

Luon stood close by, quietly looking at them.

The Egger family was finally back together again.

Shelley smiled with tears in her eyes and reached out a hand toward Luon. "Welcome back."

"It's good to see you again," Luon said, smiling back, and then he hugged them both. "I'm sorry, Shelley," he said. "I . . . can't stay, but I'll be back, and I'll tell you everything . . . I promise. And I want us to be a real family this time. I'll do whatever it takes."

"Yes, tell me everything," Shelley said through her tears. "I'll listen for as long as it takes. I don't care if it's happy or sad . . . as long as I hear it from you. Whatever problems we might have, we'll face them together, Luon." She buried her face in his shoulder.

Kip reached out from between them and grabbed Luon's hand.

"Luon?"

Luon looked down.

"Can I call you Dad now?"

"Yes," Luon said, and he picked him up in his arms.

Kip would grow into a man someday. He might grow to resent Luon for the death of his parents. But Luon had decided to be a father to Kip, and nothing would ever change that.

The three embraced for a long time, and to Edward and Alphonse, there was nothing to tell them apart from a real family.

"Thank you," Luon said at last, turning to Edward.

After a while, the time came to leave. Luon went back down the hill to the military police waiting to take him away.

Edward looked at Shelley and Kip as they waved him off, and in their faces he saw determination. They would wait for him to come home. They would wait as long as it took until they could be a family again.

"I'm glad," Alphonse said suddenly. "I know Luon might have made the wrong decisions after the massacre, but I'm glad he got a second chance."

"Yeah, me too," Edward agreed.

They may not have saved Luon from his past, but the brothers felt sure that things would improve from here on out for the Egger family.

"Say, Ed," Alphonse continued. "You know how people are always looking down on state alchemists, calling them the 'military's dogs'? I mean, I understand they have a history, and there are a lot of alchemists who don't use their power to help people . . . but I can't help thinking that if there were more alchemists who went out of their way to help, even without orders or chance of a reward, people's opinions might start to change. It might take a while, but they'd change."

"Al . . ."

"I guess I just wish there were more state alchemists like you."

Edward looked down at his open hands.

Roy and Luon would carry the memory of the massacre with them like chains around their ankles for the rest of their lives. They knew what their power was capable of—a power that Edward shared.

When he chose to become a state alchemist, Edward knew he would have to follow orders. But how would he feel if he were forced to use his powers to destroy another person's life? In fact, it didn't matter whether he used his powers or not. How would he feel if another person died or was injured because of something he'd done?

Would he give up alchemy and quit searching for a way to restore his original body? Or would he forge onward, not caring and not looking back? Edward didn't know which he would choose. He might even choose both.

Then Edward thought back to Izumi, how she had sent them off at the station after they had defied her warning not to search for Dell. It occurred to him that maybe she had meant to let them go from the very beginning. She wanted to let them see where the path they were on could lead them. She wanted them to change their course. What would Izumi say?

The lessons you teach yourself are always more important than the lessons you learn from others.

"Ed!"

Edward turned around. Alphonse was standing in front of the bookshop with Shelley and Kip, waving for Edward to join them.

"They say the train for Dublith is leaving soon."

"I'll help you pack your stuff, Edward," Kip offered.

"Thanks!"

Edward thought about getting on the train, going back to Dublith and then on to . . . where?

He didn't know where they would go next or what would be waiting for them there. He would just do what he had to in order to keep moving on toward his dream that, one day, he and his brother would have their true bodies back again.

And if it ever came time to make a choice, he would choose to be a state alchemist still—one who worked to help people, not to hurt them.

Edward took a deep breath, said a prayer for the road ahead, and looked up at the twilight sky.

It was time to catch their train. ✦

EPILOGUE

"... TAKE."

Roy sat in the officers' room at Eastern Command, sorting through his belongings.

"... Don't take."

Several days had passed since the chimera incident had finally been put to rest.

"Better leave these files for my successor . . . Don't need this book. Oh, here's that pen . . . Hmm. Out of ink."

Roy leaned forward in his chair, taking careful aim at the wastebasket in the corner. He had just tossed the pen when there came a knock at the door.

"Excuse me, sir." It was Havoc. "Mind if I come in?"

"Not at all. What's up?" Roy continued sorting, motioning Havoc into the room with a tilt of his head.

"Update on the chimera incident: That Balerea Dell fellow's regained consciousness. He's talking again too. Has a lot of colorful things to say about the academy—and us, sir. Oh, and he gave me a message for you."

"What's that?"

"To the commanding officer at Eastern: I'll never forgive what you have done to me. Consider yourself warned."

Roy glanced up at Havoc. "You haven't told him that I'm transferring?"

"Not a word, sir," Havoc said, giving a thumbs-up. Roy nodded. His successor was more than welcome to any grudges this Dr. Dell might have for him.

"Think you'll be able to wrap up that incident report, then?"

"Luon Egger is being very cooperative, so it shouldn't be a problem. Oh, and some good news: remember Brigadier General Bason? He's been demoted. They found out about some shady deals he made a few years back."

"I see."

This was good news indeed. Roy found himself liking Bason even less after the night spent at his mansion. The man was clearly overdue for some punishment.

Havoc ran through the rest of his report, then looked over the boxes and luggage piled up in the room.

"If you've got anything that can go on the freight train for Central, I'll bring it downstairs."

"That box can go, thanks."

"Yes, sir."

Havoc picked up the box and pried the door to the hallway open with his foot. He was about to leave when he stopped and turned back to Roy. "Oh, sir?"

"Hmm?"

"I know a commanding officer's got a lot of responsibilities, but you should try to look after your own skin a bit more. That's a message from all us officers here at Eastern."

Roy's eyes widened slightly.

So they *had* been worried about him out on the front lines, fighting the chimeras. He was about to offer a message of thanks in return, when Havoc spoke again.

"Not that you'll listen, sir."

"That's one message too many, Second Lieutenant," Roy said with a glare.

Havoc shrugged. "Just telling it like it is. Oh, and there's something of yours in the night-duty room. First Lieutenant Hawkeye's saying she'll throw it out if you don't come pick it up."

"W-wait!" Roy stammered. "Tell her I'll come look at it later, so don't go throwing anything out."

Havoc saluted and retreated down the hall.

Roy sighed and returned to his sorting. He would be leaving tomorrow for good, headed for Central with a handful of the officers in tow.

Through the open window, he could hear sounds of boxes and crates being placed on the bed of a waiting truck on the driveway outside.

"Hey, Colonel! Can I get your signature on this shipping label?" one of his men called from the ground below.

"Right! Coming!"

Roy closed the last box and opened the drawer to his desk. He reached in and picked up the single photograph lying inside.

"Well, I'm finally off to Central," he told his friend smiling in the photograph.

Roy had decided he would continue on up the ranks, and there would be no stopping him.

"I'll get to the top, Hughes," he said softly. "You just watch me."

Then Roy slipped the photograph into his shirt pocket, closed the empty drawer, and walked out of the room. ⚙

AFTERWORD

GREETINGS, Makoto Inoue here.

I hope you enjoyed my little intrusion into the world of Arakawa Sensei's *Fullmetal Alchemist*.

If it brought even a little smile to your face, I'm happy.

RECENT NEWS:

. . . Which is to say, more pet talk. Sorry to those of you who don't like pets, but, hey, it's an afterword, so I get to indulge a little.

Anyway, I've had this chipmunk for a while, but just this year I got my very first Java sparrow. Ever heard of them? They're the little birds that sit in the palm of your hand. She's got a black head and tail, gray wings, and a light pink stomach. She tweets and chirps and flies around the room, perching on my shoulder, yanking on my hair, sitting on my hand so she can stick her head through my fingers, and generally, she seems to like me a lot.

Actually, I have no idea how she really feels, but I like to imagine when she's tweeting she's saying "I like you, I like you," and I say "I like you" back, so it was a bit like a honeymoon for the last few months.

Note I said "was." Past tense.

Imagine my grief when I got dumped. Yes, the love affair is over.

And what did my Java sparrow have to say for herself?

"I found someone new."

And who might the culprit be? My chipmunk!

Yes, my beady-eyed lover who once sang songs of passion to me from my shoulder now has eyes only for the chipmunk in the next cage over. When I let them out at the same time, she chases him around and seems to be having the time of her life.

What about all those times you said "I like you, I like you"? Oh, the treachery . . .

So I pass my days in a dreary existence, forlorn.

(Not that my Java sparrow and chipmunk are any less cute, mind you. Oh, and if you let your pets out together, take care they don't fight.)

SO, I TOLD MY EDITOR, Nomoto, that I had bought a Java sparrow the other day, and out of the blue she asks:

NOMOTO: "Oh, do you let it inside your mouth?"
INOUE: (utterly clueless) ". . . Huh?"
NOMOTO: (nervously) ". . . Maybe I heard wrong. I thought Java sparrows were supposed to sit inside your mouth."

INOUE: (in shock) "Whaaat?! How?!"

NOMOTO: "You just open your mouth and they step in
. . . (suddenly understanding) Oh, I know, maybe it
just won't fit in yours."

. . . Um, can a Java sparrow fit in anybody's mouth?

Boy, was I surprised. Actually, I'm *still* surprised.

Do Java sparrows really like being inside people's mouths?
Somebody tell me if this is true, please . . .

In closing, let me offer a word of thanks:

There are a lot of people who make writing these *Fullmetal*
novels possible. I couldn't have made it through five volumes
if it weren't for you!

Thanks to Arakawa Sensei for always taking time out of
her busy schedule to carefully check my work.

And thanks to my editor Nomoto, whose guidance has
helped make every one of these novels much better than it
would have been without. Thanks to the publishers and the
printers, too. I couldn't do it without your help.

And finally, thanks to everyone who's been reading *Fullmetal* all along, and those of you who've just started. And a
special thanks to everyone who sends letters (They gave me the
strength to go on. Thanks so much. I read every one of them!).

Thanks to you all from the bottom of my heart! ⊕

Second floor, second stack from the right, fifth shelf from the top, two volumes.

Um, where are the dictionaries?

Up top on the second floor, five volumes.

MUMBLE

Any art history?

WHISPER WHISPER

Downstairs cellar, seventh shelf from the top on the second stack from the right, two volumes.

FLIP FLIP FLIP

Do you have any cookbooks?

MUTTER MUTTER

Twelfth book from the right: there's a first printing of Jon Einer's *Tall & Popular In Eight Easy Steps*, 1,800 cenz.

Second stack from the back, third stack from the front, second shelf from the top.

Hey, got any books on how to get taller?

YOU CHECKED THEM ALL??

Oh, and also on the second floor...

A whopping 3,200 cenz for the leatherbound deluxe version.

Oh, and on the second floor, fifth stack, bottom shelf, the twenty-eighth book from the right: Goran Deeno's *Super Tall*.

There's another in the stack of boxes on the...

FLIP FLIP FLIP FLIP FLIP FLIP

WHOA

FLIP FLIP

AFTERWORD

No matter how many times I do an afterword, I never seem to get any better at them. Thanks to Inoue Sensei and tons of other people for making this all possible!

Thanks

My own bookshelves are a mess, and I've got stacks on the floor, so boy was I jealous when I read about Ed's librarian talents in this volume!! Not to mention a place where you can just sit and read books!!!

Not to mention people who are good at writing afterwords!!!

If you were looking for a punch line, look elsewhere!

あらかわ
ひろむ

Hiromu Arakawa 6/2005